SON OF A
BITCH

ANDRE DUZA

**WRATH
JAMES WHITE**

deadite
press

DEADITE PRESS
205 NE BRYANT
PORTLAND, OR 97211
www.DEADITEPRESS.com

AN ERASERHEAD PRESS COMPANY
www.ERASERHEADPRESS.com

ISBN: 978-1-62105-114-5

Son of a Bitch © 2012, 2013 by Wrath James White and Andre Duza

Cover art copyright © 2013 Steven Gilberts

Printed in the USA.

To Mom

SON
OF A
BITCH

Demetrius didn't know what to do with the terrible little thing grinning at him from his open closet door. Creepy little fucker was freaking him out.

"Man, this shit can't be happening. This mutherfucker can't be real. I must have smoked some bad shit. Shit like this ain't supposed to be!" His mind kept screaming at him. Yet there it sat, splashing around in the blood and entrails of its mother, purring and cooing contentedly.

Helplessly, Demetrius watched as the thing tore its way out of its mother's birth canal. Ripping her wide until vagina and asshole became one gaping maw. Now the little ghoul was slowly cannibalizing her; grinning at Demetrius with its huge mandibles filled with rows of long saber teeth streaked with blood, meat, and gore. It reminded him of the time they'd caught the retarded kid down the block eating road kill.

A whimpering sound came from the thing's half-eaten mother and Demetrius shuddered and leapt backward when he realized she was still alive.

"Awww, no! Jesus Christ, no!"

Sheba was staring at Demetrius with those big puppy-dog eyes, pleading with him to help her. Every time he reached out for her, his stomach lurched in revulsion. He turned and ran into the bathroom, regurgitating into the toilet. The little ghoul just kept munching and grinning, grinning and munching.

From where Demetrius knelt with his face over the toilet bowl, he turned and watched as the thing grabbed one of her swollen tits and jerked it free sending milk and blood squirting out in a jet which it greedily knelt to consume; slurping and gobbling loudly. He could hear Sheba yelp and whimper from where she lay in that tangle of blood meat and organs being consumed by her own progeny. Another wave of nausea struck him and once again he thrust his head into the toilet bowl, a spray of projectile vomit erupted from his gut and splashed hard against the porcelain.

He had loved that dog. It had been the largest one in the whole litter and he'd sold it for eight hundred and fifty bucks

7

to the Cuban family who lived in the big white Colonial down the street. He should have known those coke-heads would have something worse than the normal mischief planned for the dog, but he'd just assumed they'd wanted her to fight or to guard their stash of illegal drugs like nearly everyone else who bought dogs from him. How the hell could he have known they were going to have sex with it?

He'd rescued it from those crazy Cubanos when he found out they were using it in some weird voodoo sex shit. It wasn't real voodoo. Nothing like what the Haitians around the corner were into. Nothing that benign. This was something much darker. He'd known lots of Yuruba and Santeria practitioners and none of them would have fucked a dog during a ritual orgy. Those perverts were into some truly demonic psychosexual shit. He should have known when Salvador showed up to pay for the dog, twitching and jerking with withdrawal symptoms, his head shaven, a goat's head pentagram tattooed on the back of his skull and a third eye tattooed on his forehead, that nothing good would come of that transaction. He should have sent the fucker packin' right then and there. But it wasn't like Demetrius to turn down money and so, against his better judgment, he'd sold Sheba to the little whack job.

As soon as he heard what they were up to, he knew he had to get her back. He'd have never sold them the dog in the first place, no matter how much money they offered, if he'd known they were going to gang rape the damned thing.

It wasn't that Demetrius was some type of animal activist. He had a kennel full of bull mastifs, pit bulls, and rottweilers. Some would wind up as combatants in any one of the many underground dog fights that proliferated all over the projects. Others would find themselves standing guard outside some drug den. Demetrius made his living by breeding and training vicious attack dogs for one criminal undertaking or another. He'd even rented mastifs to a hit man from further up north named Warlock who'd wanted to use them to dispose of a body. He generally didn't care what happened to his dogs once they were bought and paid for. But what they were doing to Sheba just wasn't right.

8

Demetrius stormed over to their house and leapt the fence into the backyard just as the high priest was busting a nut inside poor Sheba. There was a whole congregation of naked acolytes, chanting and undulating wildly to a thundering tribal drumbeat while others slaughtered chickens and cannibalized a goat in some type of perverse communion ritual. There was a woman with no eyes, just sunless pits cored into her skull, reading a bible backwards as it burned in her hands. She had a large crucifix, complete with the agonized effigy of Christ, rammed most of the way up into her hairless vagina and an understandable look of discomfort on her face. Demetrius wondered briefly how she was able to read without eyes.

Some exceptionally good weed, laced with some type of hallucinogen, smoldered in big ritual bowls all over the yard. Two more blind and naked priestesses were carving runes and symbols on a decapitated white lady who was missing her heart, and entire reproductive system. She had really nice tits though, Demetrius noticed appreciatively. Sick fuckers like these always managed to get the best pieces of ass.

Demetrius broke up the whole ritual, and took his dog back at gun-point, busting off a few shots into the sky for emphasis and chastising them all in the harshest expletives he could muster for their deviancy and lack of respect for man's best friend. He didn't care about the woman they had chained up to the tree with her head missing and her female parts cut out. That was their business. But nobody did that kind of sick shit with his dogs! He gave them their money back and told them to find another breeder to supply their sex toys.

He was still shaking with rage and revulsion when he finally got the dog home. The poor thing was frightened to death.

They had done some cutting on the dog and the stitches they had used to sew up her wounds had gotten infected. It took weeks to get the stitches to heal properly. Demetrius patiently dressed its wounds everyday and nursed poor Sheba slowly back to full strength. By the time he got the dog to stop shaking and shivering and pissing itself every time he got near it, her belly was swollen with pregnancy.

If he had known that the child belonged to one of those crazy-ass Cubanos he would have slit the dog's throat himself and buried her in the backyard. Better that than to allow this abomination to be born. But that type of stuff was not supposed to be possible. Interspecies sex was just a perverse fetish. It was not supposed to be able to produce a child.

Demetrius figured they must have done something to the dog with their sex magic and the womb they'd stolen from that woman. Still, what came out of that dog was nothing the mating of a human and a bull-mastiff could adequately account for.

You had to look closely to see either the dog or the human in it. It looked almost like a cross between a baboon, a wart hog, and a hyena. Its face was anthropoid but looked more like the pictures in fairy tale books of goblins and trolls. It kind of looked like one of the creatures in that children's book *Where The Wild Things Are.* And it gnashed its terrible teeth, and bared its terrible claws and tore its way right out of Sheba's bleeding snatch.

Demetrius sat up all night watching the little thing snack on its dead mother, wondering what the hell to do with it. He was more than a little afraid of the monster. Finally he got so mad that he scooped it up and marched back down the street to where those crazy Cubanos lived and banged on the door. Salvador answered the door, high as hell and grinning like an idiot. He stopped grinning, instead laughing hysterically when he spotted the thing Demetrius was carrying, noting the horrified look on his face.

"This shit ain't funny, man! Look at this motherfucker! What the hell is it? Damned thing just killed my dog! Tore right out of her! What the hell did you bastards do to my dog?!"

Pretty soon he had the whole family standing at the door laughing at him. He tried to give the thing back to them but they just kept laughing. They slammed the door right in his face.

"You wanted your dog back negrito? Well, you got it. You keep it!" Salvador said as he turned his back on Demetrius and walked back into the house.

After a heated argument and a few death threats shouted through the locked door, Demetrius took the little monster back home. It tried to crawl back up into its mother but Demetrius couldn't stand to see the thing snack on her any longer. He dragged her out back and buried her as deep as he could to keep the other dogs from digging her up. That freakish goblin-dog-thing yipped at his heels the whole time. It even seemed to cry when he threw the last shovel of dirt on her.

***

The next day a shadow darkened Demetrius' doorstep. A tall, emaciated scarecrow with yellow teeth and black eyes cross-hatched with an explosion of red capillaries making the whites of his eyes appear to be bleeding. He looked like he'd never slept a day in his life, like insomnia had driven him mad, wandering aimlessly day and night looking for souls to drag to hell. He was wearing a long trench coat despite the summer heat that hung loosely from his broad bony shoulders. His long dreadlocks swayed in the breeze beneath his crumpled black Panama hat. It was that hit man dude from the Eastside. Warlock. He knocked once and the goblin dog leapt at the door, nearly tearing it off the hinges trying to get at him. Demetrius had to wrestle the canine thing to the ground and slip a leash around its neck to calm it down before opening the door. The man stood on the threshold with a horrified expression on his normally stoic face. The guy was as hard as they came and it was spooking Demetrius a little to see the man looking so frightened.

"Hey, Warlock! What's going on, man?" Demetrius said. He didn't bother extending his hand as he knew the man had a thing about being touched. Demetrius watched as Warlock's features resolved themselves back into their normal stone facade. His pupils were so huge that only a sliver of his irises were visible, as if it was the middle of the night or something and not ten o'clock in the morning. The only people Meech had ever seen who'd had eyes that unresponsive were either comatose or dead.

"Uh...what the fuck was that?"

"What?"

"Fuck do you mean what? That thing that damn near took off your front door?!"

"Oh! Well it's...well...uh... I don't know what the fuck it is."

Warlock had come to see Demetrius about renting some dogs for another job. But when he saw the little monster that Demetrius was dragging around by a leash, he started to get a different idea.

"How much to borrow that for a few hours?"

"Um, I don't know man. This thing could be dangerous."

"Yeah, fool. That's the point!" Warlock replied.

The dark scarecrow leaned in close as he spoke so that Demetrius was looking right into those endless black pits and seeing himself swirling down them into some unimaginable hell. His breath steamed in Meech's face. It smelled like fetid meat as if he'd been eating carrion.

"Uh, give me two gees and we'll call it good."

"Two thousand? Just to rent him?" he asked taking a step towards Meech.

Demetrius quickly stepped back out of his reach. The goblin thing at his feet bristled and growled in warning as Warlock advanced through the doorway dragging shadows that looked like they came from several different bodies. Perhaps they were the souls of the people he'd killed. They certainly didn't belong to him. The dog-thing seemed to notice it too. His hair stood on end and he began to shake as the hit man sucked all the heat from the room with his icy stare. Demetrius tried to hold his ground but he couldn't look the corpse-like assassin in those spirit-devouring chasms that swirled down into oblivion where his eyes should have been.

"Hey bro, there's risks involved for me too. This dog could be traced back to me and then I'm an accessory in whatever shit you got planned. Besides, I suspect that he'll be doing all the work anyway. I think that's worth at least two gees."

Warlock smiled wide so that all 36 teeth were visible. He looked like a great black shark. Meech could see that some of his teeth did appear to be stained with blood. "Maybe he had started disposing of the bodies himself?" thought Demetrius with a visible shudder that seemed to make Warlock's smile widen. His eyes however remained hard and humorless if not completely vacant. If he hadn't been speaking and moving, you could almost believe the man was dead. He only appeared to breathe every now and then as if on an afterthought. And he was always perfectly still. No gestures, no shifting from foot to foot, no superfluous movement of any kind. Even the dog had quieted down and was staring at him as if he were just as fascinated by the corpse-like killer as Demetrius was.

"Here." Warlock said, handing Demetrius a roll of hundred dollar bills and snatching the leash out of his hand. He turned and walked off down the street, dragging the little goblin dog. Warlock's face once again a stoic mask.

"Weird muthafucker!" Demetrius said under his breath.

But at least that little demon is out of my hair for a few nights, he thought.

***

Demetrius never watched the news. But after a long day of cleaning kennels and slinging Purina, he needed something to take his mind off his troubles. He sat down in his living room and turned on the television, mostly just to provide background noise to drown out the sound of the Cubans up the street beating their cungas and playing their tamborines. It reminded him too much of the night he'd caught them fucking Sheba. He kept picturing them raping some other poor pooch they'd snatched off the street somewhere and he was feeling guilty for not mustering up enough give-a-fuck to go rescue the helpless thing.

"As long as it's not my dog it ain't none of my business." He said as he clicked the power button on the remote. The Sony high definition wide screen sparked to life and the silicone enhanced news whore began talking about the day's tragedies using mostly words that started with P like "prosecution", "punishment", and "perplexed" so that she could purse her big collagen lips as if she was blowing cum bubbles. Every male who watched the 6:00 news soon found himself imagining his dick in the anchorwoman's throat and his seed gargling up out of her mouth and dribbling over that cock sucker pucker as she prattled on about "perverted pedophiles" and "pernicious perps". He knew he wasn't the only one.

Today she was struggling to find the right P words to describe a string of gruesome murders in which prominent organized crime figures had been torn to bloody purple and red piles of plundered and pulverized meat, organs, and pulp.

"Awww shit naw! Warlock, what the fuck did you do?"

In a downtown Italian restaurant guys with names like Sammy "the Boar" Graciano, Nick "the Sleeper" Martucci, and Big Joey Nicollete were found strewn from one end of the joint to the other. Their shredded carcasses rent into strands of meat and viscera that were almost indistinguishable from the spaghetti with marinara sauce that sat uneaten on their plates.

"Not the usual Mafia-style gangland hit." The blowjob lady offered.

"No shit." Demetrius replied.

Oh, but it got better. Next was a scene of Jamaican and Columbian cocaine Czars tossed about a whorehouse in bite-sized chunks like wet strawberry-colored confetti surrounded by nearly a hundred kilos of coke. Then on to a street corner where leading members of The Junior Black Gangster Lords had been turned into rat food. Warlock must have used that little monster to hit every major criminal in town.

"I should have asked for a hell of a lot more than two gees," Demetrius thought to himself as he looked away from the live on-the-scene correspondent who was wiping little bloody bits of gangster off her pumps and back at the anchorwoman whose breasts were heaving as she pontificated about the carnage while hyperventilating as if she was sitting on a dick. She pursed her lips again in an absolutely lascivious pout and turned to face the camera in one of those long drawn out soap opera moments. Demetrius couldn't help it. He reached into his pants and took his growing erection firmly in hand.

"Painful." She said, blowing the word out like a kiss. They switched to a commercial and Demetrius popped *Cum Guzzling Sluts Vol. 6* into the VCR and began violently stroking his rigid flesh to scenes of faces, asses, and areolas splashed with semen from an endless procession of impossibly long cocks. He caressed his own beast, all the while trying to figure out what to do about Warlock and his dog-thing.

Demetrius had just finished wiping the cum out of his navel with a dishrag when he heard the knock on his door and the snuffling sounds of a very large animal sniffing at his threshold. He opened the door and there stood Warlock grinning like a piranha with the blood-splattered goblin-dog crouched at his heels. The dog-thing had quite a few bullet holes in it and Warlock had not even bothered to pull the switchblade out of its eye. Not that the little monster seemed to notice. He wagged his tail happily and rushed inside.

"What the fuck did you do wi—to my dog." He'd almost said "with my dog' but remembered who he was talking to and decided not to give the man any excuse to clean up witnesses.

"That's no dog." It was all Warlock said before he collapsed in the entryway in a pool of blood. His guts unraveled from his lacerated abdomen and boiled out of the hideous wound in long ropes like bloated sea slugs as he fell to his knees and then tilted over onto his face. He was still grinning just before his face hit the tile floor with a nauseating wet "Smack!"

"Fuck! Crazy fucking dog! Just look at this shit!"

The little dog thing sat grinning and wagging its tail as

15

Demetrius dragged Warlock's corpse out of the doorway, down the hall, and into the kitchen. Using only a meat cleaver and a rusted saw he began disposing of Warlock's body bit by bit. The grotesque creature sat staring up at him with big puppy-dog eyes, whimpering, as if to beg for table scraps, as Demetrius sawed through Warlock's cervical vertebrae and removed his head. He separated his radius and ulna from the humerus and dumped his forearms in there as well before sealing up that bag and opening another into which he dumped the hit man's legs. Finally he sawed through Warlock's sternum and cracked him in half putting one half of his torso in one bag and the other half in another feeling a bit queasy as he relented and tossed the man's entrails to the beast begging at his feet.

When he was done he was covered in thick tacky blood and sweat. He was too exhausted to do anything more with the body so he dumped it all into the two trashcans he kept in the garage. Tomorrow he would decide whether to risk putting the mess out on the trash or feeding it to his other dogs. He knew they would appreciate the fresh meat but he worried about them acquiring a taste for it.

"Now what the fuck am I supposed to do with this mutt?"

Demetrius took four of his pitbulls out of his smallest kennel and piled them into one of the larger cages with six other pitbulls. They would probably fight and one or two of them might even wind up dead but that was still better odds than if he stuck this little goblin dog in there with them. He shuffled the beast into the empty kennel and padlocked the door. Then he dragged his own tired ass back into the house, locked the back door, locked and barricaded his bedroom door, and collapsed on his bed, fully dressed, into a fitful sleep filled with dreams of cops storming his door, that weird ass dog gulping down Mafia kingpins like kibble, and that creepy ass hit man returning from the grave.

"Wake up, fool! Get your ass out that bed!"

It was Warlock's voice. It had to be a dream.

"Muthafucka, I said get your ass out that bed!"

Something wet slapped tight around his wrist and

dragged him off the bed and onto the floor.

"What tha fuck?"

When Demetrius looked up he screamed his throat raw and passed out.

***

"Wake up! Wake the fuck up! Stop bein' a little pussy would you? We ain't got time for this shit!"

Demetrius woke up and once again saw the little goblin dog standing over top of him speaking to him with Warlock's gravely voice. He opened his mouth to scream.

"You scream again and I'll bite your face off. I swear to God I will. Now shut the fuck up and pay attention."

"Warlock? Is that you in there?"

"What the fuck do you think? What were you thinking letting this muthafucker eat my heart?"

He said it like Demetrius should have somehow known that feeding his heart to his demonic pet would have transferred the hitman's soul into the dog's body.

"You were dead, man. I was just trying to get rid of the body. How the fuck was I supposed to know?"

"You destroyed my body?"

"Well…yeah. I mean… you weren't breathing or nothing and half your guts were hanging out. You were fucking dead, man! How the fuck can I be talking to a dead man?"

Demetrius watched the hideous dog thing's mouth move to shape words in Warlock's voice and it was the creepiest thing he could remember seeing. As fascinating as it was nauseating.

"You really in there, Warlock?"

"Yeah, I'm in here. So tell me about my body? Did you feed my whole body to this little monster of yours?"

"No…um…just your insides. You know…just your guts and organs and stuff. I didn't want the thing running around the house hungry. I mean, I heard on the news what the thing did to those Mafia dudes and I mean, look what it did to you. I didn't want it getting' hungry and turning on me…"

17

Demetrius recognized that stoic expression as the goblin dog's face darkened and hardened. Its eyes turned black and cold like Warlock's had been as it leaned in and growled in Demetrius' ear.

"You don't know shit about what happened to those Mafia dudes, you dig? You don't know shit about that. So just keep your fuckin' mouth shut about that shit!"

"Okay! Okay! It ain't like you can go to jail for that shit no way. You're already dead. They ain't gonna lock a dog up for life."

"No. But they do euthanize animals that kill people."

"Oh. Yeah. Right."

"So you just forget all about what you saw on the news. We got more pressing shit to deal with. You said you fed my organs to the dog? Hmmm? Well those can be replaced. What did you do with the rest of me?"

Replaced? How? What the fuck was he talking about?

"The rest of you?"

"Yeah, muthafucka I ain't stutter! What did you do with the rest of me?"

"I…um…I cut it up."

"You what?"

"I cut it up and threw it in the trash."

"Shit! You stupid son of a bitch!"

"Well how the fuck was I supposed to know? I thought you were dead! Muther fucker you *are* dead! Why the fuck do you care what I did with your body?"

"You're gonna have to find me a new one."

"What?"

"Did I stutter? You've got to find me a new body! You get me a body. You take me down the street to the Cubans and they'll take care of the rest."

"The Cubanos? You fuckin' around with those weird mutherfuckers and their Voodoo shit? That's how all this shit started! Those freaky sons of bitches fucked my dog!"

"Just shut the fuck up and get dressed."

Warlock crawled off of Demetrius' chest. Demetrius sat up and then scooted up the wall staring at the dog, wondering

18

if all of this was just some bad hallucination. Unfortunately he was not high. He didn't do anything stronger than weed and he'd never had a hallucination from smoking the chronic. Today he hadn't even smoked any weed. He'd have to correct that soon. No way he was gonna get through this day without a little herb to keep his head straight.

"Hurry the fuck up, fool! I don't want to stay like this forever!"

"Yeah. Right. My fault. Just let me get some shoes on and change my shirt. You…um drooled all over this one."

Demetrius stood and walked over to the closet, stepping over piles of porn magazines, DVDs and VHS tapes, pizza boxes, soda and beer cans, and Chinese Food cartons. He ducked his head into the closet and reached over the mountainous pile of dirty clothes to retrieve the one clean T-shirt he had left. It was a black heavy metal T-shirt with "Megadeth" emblazoned across the front. He had no idea where he'd gotten it from. He'd never even heard of the group. Yet, somehow it felt appropriate. In the last twenty-four hours he had been surrounded by mega amounts of death and gore and the body count would likely keep rising until he found a body for Warlock to possess or whatever the fuck he planned on doing with it.

Demetrius led Warlock out of the house. He was holding a leash in his hands, trying to decide how to ask Warlock if he could put it on him.

"What the fuck is your ass doing with that leash?"

"I just thought it might make people more comfortable if you were on a leash or something. Seeing you walking around like that might freak people out. I mean, this thing was ugly before, but now it's… you're… all shot up and cut up and missing an eye. You're about the ugliest looking thing I've ever seen! You'll scare the hell out of people walking around like this!"

"We ain't walkin', fool! My Escalade's right outside. You didn't check my body for the keys before you hacked it up and fed it to this ugly mutt of yours?"

"Yeah…I…um I put them in the freezer with your

wallet."

"In the freezer? Fuck would you put keys in the freezer for?"

"I don't know. In case someone came looking for you or something they probably wouldn't look in there. I've got one of those old freezers that's all covered with frost and shit. You can't find nothin' in there."

"Well, you'd better find my keys motherfucker and let's get going!"

Demetrius ran back into the kitchen, looking over his shoulder at his murderous pet that was now possessed by the spirit of a notorious hitman.

"How tha fuck did I get my black ass into this mess?"

He retrieved the keys and walked out the front door with Warlock.

"My Cadi is right around the corner."

Demetrius felt self-conscious walking down the street with the hideous talking canine.

"I hope nobody thinks I bred you. That would fuck up my whole rep as a breeder if they see your ugly ass."

"You did breed this ugly mutt, fool! And it ain't like your ass was gunning for a spot in the British Kennel Club. You breed pit bulls and Rotts for dog fights and guard dogs. Don't get the shit twisted, yo. None of your dogs are going to wind up in the Westminster Dog Show any time soon."

"Man, keep your voice down before somebody hears you. How the fuck am I going to explain a talking dog with bullet holes in him?"

"Relax. Ain't nobody out in the streets this early in the morning except crackheads and they see weirder shit than this every day."

"Hey, maybe we can snatch up one of them and stick you in their body?"

The dog stopped in its tracks and turned to look at Demetrius, snarling. The expression was not too dissimilar from the one Warlock had frequently worn when he was alive.

"Listen motherfucker! You ain't puttin' me in no

crackhead's body! You are going to find me a body better than the one I had. I've got a cousin who's like a high school basketball star only he's got fucked up grades so he probably won't ever make it to college. Find that motherfucker and we'll take his body."

"Your own cousin? That's cold, man."

"Everybody says he looks just like I did when I was a kid. This might just work out for the best. I get to go back to my youth."

The idea of a young revitalized Warlock was scarier even than one trapped in the body of a hellhound. Demetrius had done some terrible things in his day, or provided the means for others to do terrible things. He'd sold guns and even explosives on a few occasions. He'd tried selling drugs but had kept getting robbed and having to come out of his own pocket to pay off his suppliers. He'd bought his first pit bulls to guard his stash of drugs and guns. That's when he'd decided to go into the breeding business. It was safer, or so he thought. Now, he wasn't so sure he wouldn't have been better off selling Uzis and weed out of the back of his trunk.

They climbed into Warlock's big midnight black Cadillac Escalade with the spinning rims and limo tinted windows just as the first wave of nine-to-fivers shuffled out of their homes to start the daily grind.

"This is a nice ass ride, Yo! What's up with this cheap stereo though? Where's the sub woofers? If I had this thing I'd have enough speakers in here to have the whole block bumpin'!"

"Now why the fuck would a hitman want to have a stereo system that announced his ass from three blocks away?"

"True. I'd at least have DVDs in the headrest though. So, bitches could sit back there and watch pornos and shit while I cruised they asses back to my crib. I'd have this thing pimped out!"

"Nobody rides in the backseat of this mutherfucker unless they're already dead. Now shut tha fuck up and drive!"

"Uh…which way."

"Just get on the freeway. He lives down in West Philly."

Demetrius was surprised by how easy it was becoming to engage in conversation with a dog that looked like someone pumped it full of steroids and then marched it across a battlefield. The eye that had been punctured with a switchblade was starting to ooze some pink and yellow liquid down Warlock's face. He kept licking at it absentmindedly with that enormous tongue that was bigger than Demetrius' entire hand. Demetrius wanted to say something to him about how disgusting that shit was but decided that it was probably best to ignore it. Some of the bullet holes in his face, neck, and torso had scabbed over already but others looked infected and were starting to weep a clear pus that smelled like sewage. The more terrified and disgusted Demetrius became the more he talked. They discussed religion:

"So what's up with this voodoo shit you're into with the Cubanos?"

"Shut tha fuck up and drive."

They discussed politics:

"Man, shit's been fucked up ever since those damn republicans got in office. If Reagan and Bush had never gotten elected I bet neither of us would be doin' the shit we doin' now. We wouldn't even be in this situation. You runnin' around stuck in the body of some ugly-ass demon dog, smellin' like you ain't had a bath since Christ wore diapers. I mean, how you supposed to pull females lookin' like that? Female *dogs* maybe. I bet you could pull some real bitches now. You know what I'm sayin'? *Real* bitches."

"Shut tha fuck up and drive."

They talked about women:

"Hey, you ever have to smoke some really fine ass honey and you know, she offers to give you some pussy to let her live? I bet that shit happens all the time huh? What's it feel like to fuck some bitch and then smoke her? I bet that's a trip huh? I don't think I could merc some female after I'd bust a nut in her. Especially not if that shit was good. That would fuck me up to have to waste some bitch who had that bomb-ass pussy. You ever had to do that shit?"

"I'm gonna bite your nuts off, rip your fuckin' head off,

and spit your sack down your throat if you don't shut tha fuck up right now."

"Ewww! Man, that's a nasty ass image. You sick dude."

"Shut the fuck up!"

Warlock was growling at him low in his throat as he spoke. It made his voice a rumbling raspy tenor. What you'd imagine a bulldog's voice would sound like if he'd been smoking unfiltered cigarettes for a decade and drinking wood shavings.

Warlock had that look on his face that Demetrius had seen killers wear when they were pointing a gun at someone and giving them the chance to decide their fate. Demetrius had known a lot of killers in his day. He'd always made it a point to avoid being on the opposite end of that look. Only Warlock didn't need a gun anymore. Now, he could take Demetrius' head off with one bite. Demetrius turned back to the road and they drove the rest of the way in silence.

They exited the freeway in West Philly with Demetrius now nibbling his fingernails and spitting them over his shoulder and Warlock doing his best to ignore it and concentrate on what had to be done.

"Will you cut that shit out?! That's fucking nasty! And you're getting your fingernails all over my ride!"

"*I'm* nasty? Yo, have you looked in the mirror lately? Your face looks like a Sloppy Joe."

"That's it. I'm killing your ass right now. I don't care if I have to drive this mutherfucker with my damn paws!"

"Okay, okay, I'll chill. Damn, don't be so sensitive."

They stopped in front of a ten-story tenement building in the projects and Demetrius started to reach across to open the passenger side door then thought better of it. He didn't want his hands anywhere near Warlock's jaws. He jumped out of the SUV and ran around to open the door from the outside.

"You'd better clean all those fingernails out of the backseat when we're done here."

"Don't trip, man. It's all good."

"It'll be all good when I get me a new body and you get

my ride cleaned out the way you found it."

He scowled humorlessly and Demetrius wondered if that face was even capable of a joyous expression. He looked at the huge jowls dripping long ropes of drool, the jutting saber like teeth, that wide flat anthropoid nose that looked like Micheal Jackson's before his first rhinoplasty, that big black reptilian eye, and doubted it. The thing was too ugly to look cheerful.

"Your nephew lives up in here?"

"Yeah, ninth floor."

"Damn. I hate going into the projects."

"Ain't nothing in there worse than me."

Demetrius looked at Warlock who stared back at him with his one good eye. A piece of steel was still sticking out of his other eye from the blade someone had jammed into it.

True dat, he thought. *This ugly mutherfucker definitely has a point there.*

He walked up to the front door of the projects and crackheads parted like the red sea as he stepped inside with Warlock leading the way.

Demetrius cursed again and again as they walked up the seemingly endless flights of stairs on their way to the ninth floor.

"I still don't see why we couldn't have taken the elevator. I got bad knees."

"Look around you, fool. How often do you suppose the maintenance man pops into this mutherfucker? You want to get stuck in that elevator for a month or two then go ahead with your bad ass."

Demetrius tried his best to keep his complaining to a minimum as they climbed the remaining flights of stairs. It was obvious that Warlock was in a mood. He wasn't having a very good day.

They came to the eighth floor and Warlock led the way to his nephew's apartment.

"Now look, fool. My nephew is probably armed and he don't know you, so listen to what I'm telling you if you don't want to wind up with a hole in your chest."

"I'm listening."

"Just knock on the door and tell him that I sent you to pick him up. Tell him... tell him that I'm fucked up and I need his help but not to tell his momma or nobody."

Demetrius knocked on the door. He knocked twice more before the door finally creaked open and the barrel of a gun pointed through the gap between the door and the jamb.

"Who you?"

"You Warlock's cousin? Mooky?"

"My name's Maurice. Don't nobody call me Mooky but friends and family and you ain't neither. Now da fuck do you want up in here?"

"Your uncle sent me to pick you up. He needs your help, man, and if I don't bring you back with me he gonna kill me."

"My uncle don't need nobody's help. He ain't never needed nobody's help."

"He said he'd pay you and that it wasn't nothing deep. Nothing that would fuck up your scholarship or anything. He just got himself hurt and he can't move around too well and he can't let nobody see him like that... you know... the man's got enemies who might take advantage of him in his current state. He just wants you to kick it at his place for a couple of weeks until he's up on his feet, run some errands for him and shit. You can even drive his Escalade while he's healing up."

"His Escalade? Word?"

"Yeah. He can't drive it himself right now anyway."

"So what's wrong with him? He get shot or something?"

"Naw, I think he just pulled a hamstring or a groin muscle or something. He's just real self-conscious about that shit and don't want nobody to see him while he's less than one hundred percent. He said he needs family around to take care of him."

"I can dig that. But what's up with that big ugly ass dog? That thing is huge! What's it like two hundred pounds? I ain't never seen a damn dog that big. And why is it all fucked up like that? Looks like somebody kicked the shit out of him."

"He was just in a dog fight. That's what I do. I breed dogs for fighting and stuff."

"So how do you know my uncle?"

"I've known him forever. He's even bought a few dogs off of me. Don't ask me what he does with them."

"So if you so tight with him then why ain't you taken care of his ass?"

"That nigga don't trust nobody. The only reason he's trustin' me to pick you up is because he knows I'm scared of him."

"Where's the Escalade?"

"Downstairs."

"He let you drive it?" Maurice asked, his eyebrows furrowing and his eyes narrowing in suspicion.

"He ain't have no choice. I ain't got no ride. Besides, he'd smoke my ass if I scratched it or anything. He knows it's safe with me."

"Yeah? I ain't sure about this. How do I know you didn't kill his ass and steal his ride and now you tryin' to get me too?"

The long lanky teen looked past Demetrius into the hall. Then he looked long into Demetrius's eyes, trying to decide if he should trust the man or not. He tapped him on the chest with the barrel of his pistol.

"Look at me, bro. Do I look like I could take out Warlock?"

Maurice looked him over from head to toe and Demetrius knew exactly what the boy saw. The fear in his eyes, his nervous habit of swaying back and forth when he spoke and shifting from one foot to the other, his out of date clothing. He looked more like a homeless crackhead than some kind of hitman. Maurice relaxed slightly.

"You try anything funny and I swear I'm gonna peel your cap back."

"Now, you sound like your uncle. Ya'll don't trust nobody. I feel you though. The only thing I trust is my dogs." Demetrius said, patting Warlock on his head which made him growl. Demetrius pulled his hand back quickly before

26

he lost it down the big canine's throat.

With Warlock quietly observing from the backseat, Demetrius thought it best to keep the conversation to a minimum during the drive to the hitman's place. Maurice, on the other hand, was feeling especially talkative. Shifting from one topic to the next at a schizophrenic pace, he left Demetrius with no time to respond before he was off on some completely unrelated tangent. He talked about the bitches he had fucked, and how they couldn't get enough of his magic stick. He talked about his baller status at school and how everybody, even some of the teachers, was jealous of him. He talked about his long-term goals; to keep dem ends rollin' in by any means necessary.

Demetrius wanted to swerve into oncoming traffic rather than listen to one more word of the boy's immature braggadocio. He could see, via fleeting glances in the rearview, that Warlock shared his disgust. They were having their own silent conversation on the sneak. It went something like this:

"This nephew of yours doesn't know when to shut the fuck up."

"Yeah... What the fuck you want me to do about it?"

Demetrius turned on the radio and focused on the road to tune out Maurice's voice.

A short time later Demetrius caught himself nodding his head to some Godawful song that he would've turned off after only a few chords had he been paying attention. Maurice was nodding too, and with conviction. Demetrius stopped nodding and made a face at the boy. He looked and saw Warlock shaking his head at him from the rearview.

"What tha fuck!" Maurice said.

"What?" Demetrius replied, startled by the sudden outburst.

"The dog..." He didn't know how to finish the sentence. "Didju see that shit?"

"See what shit?"

Maurice wasn't comfortable repeating the sentence that his mind suggested as a response; that the goblin dog made a human face at him, like he had said or done something to piss off the ugly thing. It happened quickly, in the blink of an eye. But he was sure that he saw it. As sure as there's stink on shit. Canine facial musculature wasn't capable of conveying that kind of subtly. And there was something so familiar in the disparaging expression that Maurice thought for a second that someone he knew was sitting in the back seat. The identity of that someone lay just beyond recollect's reach.

"You ah-ight man?" Demetrius asked. He was trying to play it off like he wasn't afraid that the boy was on his way to unraveling his and Warlock's scheme. His mind was chastising him for even considering the possibility. *Like someone's gonna just figure out that their uncle's soul is trapped in a dog.*

Maurice glanced over his shoulder at the goblin dog in the backseat and then turned back around shaking his head.

"Goddamn that thing is ugly. Got me over here trippin'-n-shit. You know how dogs be lookin' at chu like a person sometimes?"

"You must be smokin' that goooood shit, hunh?"

"Naw, for real, doh."

"I'm just fuckin' with you, man. Of course I know what chor sayin'. I breed the muthafuckahs. Remember?"

"Man… For a second there I was like, 'Who da fuck is this nigga sittin' behind me?'"

Demetrius laughed. He glanced in the rearview and met Warlock's droll, one-eyed glare dead on.

"So, Unk must be slippin' in his old age, hunh?" Maurice asked after a quiet span.

"Ah…I wouldn't say that," Demetrius nervously replied.

"I-on't-know, bra. Tha muthafuckah used to be like a superhero to me when I was a kid. I remember when dem niggas from Germantown tried to take him out back in '96. My moms let him lay low in the empty apartment next to ours while he recovered. He came over right after it happened. Clothes all bloody-n-shit. And this muthafuckah was actin' like it was nothing. Now he laid up with a pulled hamstring-n-shit."

Warlock growled at Maurice's back.

"Yo, man!" Maurice yelled as he thrust his torso forward away from the seat rest. "Handle that muthafuckah before I bus-a-cap in his ugly ass!"

"Down boy! Down!" Demetrius winked at Warlock as he pretended to scold him.

Warlock backed down.

"Okay. He's cool." Demetrius said to Maurice.

"That's a big muthafuckah, man. I ain't tryin' to get bit."

"He's cool, man. Trust me."

Maurice eventually relaxed and sat back.

"I remember that night, though," Demetrius said attempting to steer the conversation back on track. "That night when Warlock got shot up. Your uncle's still a bad muthafuckah, man. Don't let his age fool you."

"Maybe it's time for the next generation to take over," Maurice replied, half-serious.

"What? You mean you? Nah man. You ain't cut out for this kinda life."

"How tha fuck you know?! You don't know me like that, nigga!"

"Whoa! Calm down, youngbuck. I ain't tryin' ta say nothing. I'm just sayin'. I know enough about you to know that you're still in school. Plus, ain't there some college lookin' at you for a basketball scholarship?"

"Yeah. Temple."

"Awwww shit! The Owls?"

"Be better if it was Georgetown or Duke or somethin'."

"Still, you do well at Temple and that's a ticket to the NBA right there. You know the kind of cheddar them muthafuckahs pull?"

Seduced by the idea of wealth and fame, Maurice's face melted dumb as he stared out the windshield fantasizing.

The Escalade crept up the driveway and into the garage of the recently constructed, two-story home in the Northern Liberties section of North Philly where Warlock stayed when he wasn't on a job. His primary residence was a shabby loft apartment situated above an out-of-business auto repair garage where he kept his "company car," (an 89 Buick Hooptie) parked and covered with a grease-stained tarp.

Northern Liberties was a gentrified pocket of young (mostly white) wealth bordered by varying degrees of inner-city machinations to the east, west, and north. The house was one of an entire block of new homes built on top of an old, trash-strewn lot where the occasional body was found back in the day. It was common for the people around here to use their garages as the sole entrance and exit, so you could go for months without ever seeing the person two doors down from you. That's what Warlock was counting on when he bought the place. He had instructed Demetrius, who then instructed Maurice, to do the same.

The house was sparsely furnished. Warlock had grown accustomed to sitting in cramped, uncomfortable places for extended periods of time while surveilling his marks. Most of the time, he preferred the floor to a couch or a dining room table. He slept on a small, loveseat-sized futon. It was the only piece of furniture in his bedroom.

Maurice complained about the lack of furniture until he saw the 49" Samsung Flatscreen mounted on the wall above the fireplace. There were several neat stacks of DVDs on the mantle below it.

"Now that's what I'm talkin' about," he said rubbing his palms together. "March Madness starts tomorrow."

"I'm gonna call your unc…" Demetrius said from the kitchen where he stood holding his cell phone. Warlock sat on the floor beside him. He was tethered to Demetrius' wrist by a short, nylon leash.

"Wha'd ju say?" Maurice replied.

Demetrius put the cell phone in his pants pocket in a manner that made him look guilty.

"Ahh… Nothing."

Maurice squinted at him and then went back to his tour of the first floor of Uncle Warlock's place.

"I'm supposed to be here, dumbass," Warlock scolded Demetrius in a whispered growl. "What'd you forget already?"

They had discussed a rudimentary plan on the walk up the stairs to Maurice's apartment.

"Just tell him that I'm upstairs in my room and that I don't wanna be bothered."

Speaking from the side of his mouth, Demetrius replied, "He's gonna figure out that you're not here, man."

"I'll be up there with the door closed, stoo-pid. I'll yell down or something so he knows."

"How are we gonna get you up there without him seeing?"

The staircase leading up to the second floor was located in the living room. Maurice was in there looking out the window.

"Looks awfully white out there," Maurice commented to Demetrius, who wasn't listening.

"See that closet over there?" Warlock said. "The one next to the fridge?"

The closet wasn't easy to find. It had a narrow door that was made to blend in with the rest of the large wood panels that decorated the wall.

"There's a hidden compartment in the back. Leads up to my bedroom. I had it put in when I first got the place. Tell that fool to chill while you run some errands."

'Run some errands' was code for tracking down Salvador and somehow convincing him to help them transfer Warlock's soul into Maurice's body. Demetrius had no idea how he was going to do that. His last interaction with the crazy muthafuckah had ended badly.

"You can tell him I just got some albino porn DVDs. That should keep him occupied. He's into that shit. Then act like you're taking me with you out to the truck."

"What the fuck is albino porn?"

"*The White Stuff? Do The White Thing?* They're black bitches but they're albino so it's like they've got white skin but still have big asses and big dick-suckin' lips. I ain't really into the shit, but I've got a couple DVDs. That fool has a ton of it at his crib."

"Albino porn, hunh? There's something wrong about

that shit. It seems like some kind of racist self-hatred shit. I mean, I like white bitches too but there's something twisted about jacking off to white black bitches. Like it's the color of their skin that turns you on or something. I'm more a Phat White Asses man, myself. You ever seen Gianna Michaels? Those tits are crazy!"

"Muthafuckah, I don't care! Now, did you get all that!?"

"I got it! I got it!"

"D'ju say something?" Maurice asked from the living room.

Demetrius just stood there, looking stupid. Warlock whacked him in the leg with his paw when Maurice looked away for a second.

"I was jusssst... talking to the dog."

He leaned over and pretended to pet the ugly beast.

"Isn't-nat right, boy," he said in the kind of voice people use with cute animals and babies.

Warlock snatched his head away and growled.

"Damn, homes!" Maurice joked. "You better get that muthafuckah in check. You gotta dominate them niggas."

"Yeah. Thanks for the advice Cesar Milan."

"Who?"

"Forget it.

Since he didn't know the reference, Maurice was suspicious. His eyes questioned: *Are you tryin' to say I'm stupid or something*? Shortly after a smile broke through his leering, lingering gaze. As he turned back to the window, Maurice snickered and said to himself, "This muthafuckah got jokes-n-shit."

"Don't ever touch me again!" Warlock growled.

"Sor-ree."

"Now listen. There's some of that albino porn in with the DVDs. Just tell him to check 'em out. He'll find it."

Demetrius took a moment to prepare, and then said to Maurice, "Why don't you just chill for a while. Get comfortable. I'm gonna take Warlo... I mean the dog with me to run some errands." He pointed to the stacks of DVDs on the floor. "Your uncle said you can watch whatever you want, by the way."

Maurice walked over and grabbed the remote control from the mantle above the fireplace. He turned on the TV and started thumbing through channels.

Demetrius waited until Maurice was safely immersed in the ambush of moving images, and then he unclipped the nylon leash from the collar around Warlock's thick, muscular neck. He tiptoed over to the closet and pulled the door open.

"Gimme about 30 seconds," Warlock whispered as he entered the closet.

Demetrius closed the door behind him and then tiptoed across the kitchen toward the larger door on the other side of the room that led to the garage. He stopped when he saw Maurice walking up the stairs.

"Hey! What'r you doing?"

Maurice stopped halfway between the first and second floors and returned a strange look.

"I'm gonna go say 'Whazzup," to Unk. Why?"

"Nah, man! He said he doesn't wanna be bothered. Plus, he's prolley sleeping right now."

Maurice thought for a second and then came back down the steps. He sensed anxiety in Demetrius' rushed demeanor and it made the boy wary of trusting him.

"He said for you to just chill for a while."

"I don't even really know you, homie for you to be handin' out orders like we in the fuckin' army or something. How do I know this shit ain't—"

"Why don't we just ask him," Demetrius blurted following his gut reaction, which then instructed him to walk into the living room and yell up the stairs to Warlock. "Yo Warlock!"

"I thought you said he didn't wanna be bothered?"

Warlock didn't answer.

Demetrius ignored the boy and tried again. He was worried that Warlock might have overestimated his new body's deftness. What if he was having trouble getting up to his room? What if he had gotten himself stuck in the secret compartment?

"YO! WARLOCK! IT'S MEECH!"

"What, Goddammit!" Warlock's muffled voice came back. "I told you I didn't wanna be bothered!"

"WHAZZUP, UNK!" Maurice yelled up the stairs.

"Sup, Mooky."

"HEY, IT'S COOL IF MAURICE WATCHES TV DOWN HERE AND CHECKS OUT YOUR DVDs, RIGHT?"

"I don't give a fuck! Just don't be choking your shit in my house."

"There you go," Demetrius said to the boy as if he had won a bet.

"Why the fuck would I do that?" Maurice asked under his breath.

"What? Choke your shit?"

"Yeah."

Demetrius shrugged, feigning ignorance.

***

Maurice was feeling some kind of way that he couldn't just bust a nut and be done with it. He was more than ready, and the material (A big-bootied albino chick slurping and slobbering all over some random dude's thick, chocolate dick) was just right. Each time Maurice came close to blowing his load into the paper towel that he held over the head of his considerably smaller dick, the scene would cut to a shot of the random dude's reaction or of his hairless ass thrusting at the albino chick's face like he meant her harm. He was palming the back of her head and forcing her to take his full length into her mouth, which she gladly accepted over and over.

It was hard enough maintaining a hard-on with Unk upstairs. He had taken precautions. He had the sound on the TV turned way down. The remote lay within reach of his left hand. A second paper towel lay directly to his right to wipe the excess Vaseline, dick-sweat, and pre-cum that he had stroked into a thick, gooey paste, from his hand. Maurice preferred to take his pants and shoes off during a

34

good stroke-session, but he left them both on this time. His throbbing dick was sticking through his unzipped fly. Every once and awhile it rubbed up against the zipper's teeth. He hated that.

Maurice heard a noise from upstairs. It was Unk's voice followed by an animal sound. Like something a dog would make. He snatched up the remote and paused the DVD while still mildly stroking his pulsating shaft. He pointed his ear at the top of the stairs and listened.

A rolling, rumbling growl turned into Unk's voice. He was moaning and making strange vocal sounds from deep in his throat. It reminded Maurice of someone in the throes of a nightmare. The growl was distinctly canine and there was no doubt that Unk's voice had come on the same breath, and from the same source. But that didn't make sense. By now, Maurice's dick had gone limp in his hand.

He heard a dog bark. He recognized the tenor of its voice now. It was that busted dog that muthafuckah Demetrius had with him.

What the fuck is going on here?

"Goddamn paws! Can't do a thing with 'em!" Warlock yelled, his voice still muffled by the bedroom door.

Maurice wiped the gooey paste from his hand with the paper towel. He then wrapped the soiled paper towel around his flaccid penis, squeezed, and then slid his hand up toward the head. Then he stuffed it back into his pants and zipped them up. Stepping lightly, he walked up to the foot of the staircase and listened.

"Swear ta God if you try ta pet me again I'll bite your muthafuckin' arm off!" Warlock growled.

Maurice crept up the stairs to investigate.

"That's right I can talk! S'what I've been trying to tell you!"

Unk's bedroom was the first room on the right. The door was slightly cracked. Maurice crept up to the door, crouched in front of it, and peeked inside.

The room looked like it hadn't been lived in for months. Demetrius' goblin dog was sleeping on the floor with its back to the door. It was breathing heavily and whimpering. The goblin dog shifted its weight and rolled over. Maurice nearly shit his pants. The thing flinched and stirred before it finally settled into a comfortable position. Its eye was closed the entire time. Yellow-green fluid had hardened to a crust as it oozed from the mangled pit where its other eye used to be. After a few seconds it started to snore. Then Maurice saw the thing's right hand and forearm. Both were unmistakably human.

"I'm a man, Goddammit!"

Maurice froze. He had clearly witnessed the goblin dog's lips moving to shape words. The beast's entire face was vested in the response. He saw a fleeting resemblance to Unk in the way its features wrinkled and scrunched.

"A MAN!"

Maurice screamed and fell on his ass. He hit the door with his feet as he kicked his legs out and pushed himself backward. He smacked his head on the wall behind him and knocked himself momentarily dizzy.

The bedroom door swung open. The ugly goblin dog was on its feet.

"Maurice!" Warlock said. He took a step toward the boy and stopped suddenly. Something didn't feel right. He looked down and shuddered at the human hand and forearm at the end of his right leg. The palm was flat against the floor. The fingers were flexed and spread. The forearm was bulbous and oddly muscular in contrast with the skinny canine leg that connected it to his shoulder. The back of the hand was decorated with plump veins and deep, linear striations in the muscle. Wiry digits were tipped with overgrown human fingernails.

"OH FUCK!" Warlock cried out and stumbled sideways away from the strange new appendage. He fell and rolled clumsily onto his back. His legs flailed at the ceiling. He smacked his palm down on the floor and used it to regain his footing. Standing on three wobbly doglegs, he held the hand up to his face, stared quizzically, and whined, "WHAT THE FUCK IS THIS SHIT!?" Then he remembered Maurice and looked up at the boy.

"Don't fuckin' come near me, muthafuckah!" Maurice warned as he slid his feet beneath him and stood up. He snatched his gun from his belt, pointed it at Warlock...

"Maurice, wait!"

...and squeezed the trigger twice. One of the bullets smacked Warlock in the shoulder and sent him reeling backward. Afterward Maurice took off running toward the stairs.

Warlock groaned at the pain in his shoulder and then limped after his nephew.

"MAURICE! WAIT! IT'S ME! IT'S UNK!"

***

"A hand!?"

"A human-f-u-c-k-i-n-g-hand, Yo!"

"I don't get it."

"Muthafuckah, you think I do? All I know is I woke up and there it was."

Demetrius' attention was divided between Warlock's voice on the other end of the phone and the team of agitated-looking police officers that congregated in front of Warlock's house. The front door was hanging open and spitting out and swallowing more officers. A small crowd of nosey spectators had gathered in the street beyond the blockade of police cars. The Escalade was parked a block away. Demetrius was sitting in the driver seat holding his cell phone to his ear and looking worried as he stared through the windshield.

"What tha fuck's goin' on, man!? There's cops everywhere out here!"

"Cops?! Where?!"

"Outside your place! Don't tell me you're still in there?!"

"Fuck! FUCK!" Warlock took a moment to assimilate the new twist into his thought process, and then said, "Did you get a hold of Salvador, at least?"

"I tried, but nobody answered the door. Where are you?"

Demetrius didn't really knock on Salvador's door. He had driven to the Cuban's house earlier, but then just cruised around the block a few times trying to come up with some way to reason with the crazy bastard and coming up empty.

"I'm hiding in the bushes on North Broad."

"Tha fuck'r you doin' there?! Where's Maurice?"

"He's dead."

"Wha?! You killed him?"

"No! Five-O got 'em. The noozie muthafuckah snuck up to my room, bugged out, and started blastin' away when he saw me. Then he ran like a bitch. I tried to catch him but he was too fast. Plus this fuckin' hand kept trippin' me up. Stupid muthafuckah was running down the street bussin' off caps at me like a damn fool."

Demetrius didn't need to hear the rest. A black man running down the street firing a gun? It wasn't too hard to figure out how it went down from that point.

"I was coming back to my place when the fuckin' dogcatchers, three-a-them muthafuckahs, came outta nowhere and choked me up with them poles with a rope at the end and threw me in their truck. I was so tired from chasin' Maurice's bitch ass that I didn't have the strength to fight them off. I made a break for it when they got back to that shelter on Erie Avenue and tried to get me out. Jumped right out that mothafuckah and knocked this hippy nigga on his ass. Bit the shit out that muthafuckah, too. I think I swallowed a couplahis fingers."

Demetrius paused to digest the information. *No way this ain't gonna end badly. No fucking way.* He glanced at the LCD screen on his cell phone remembering that he didn't recognize the number when the phone rang 10 minutes ago.

"What'r you calling from, a payphone?"

"Nah. I swiped that hippy nigga's cellie. It fell out of his pocket when I jumped on 'em."

"You alright, man?" Demetrius half-hoped that he wasn't alright. That way he would be done with this whole crazy mess.

"I'm a fucking dog! No, I'm not alright!"

"Shit, man! What're you gonna do now?"

"*WE* are gonna get my ass a new body. I think I might

actually have somebody in mind."

"Who?"

Warlock was looking through an opening in the row of thick bushes at a badly faded billboard across the street. A stalwart, barrel-chested Caucasian man wearing a leather jacket, stood with his arms crossed glaring down from the billboard at the little people who mucked about in the street below. Bold lettering hovered over him and threatened: COMMIT A CRIME WITH A HANDGUN IN PHILLY, GET A MANDATORY FIVE YEARS IN PRISON!

"Victor Dom."

Victor Dom was a hotshot homicide detective known for his tough stance against violent criminals. He was a thorn in the side of Organized Crime back in the 80s. Since orchestrating their downfall, he had turned his attention to the black community. He was single-handedly responsible for taking down some of Warlock's competition.

Although the idea of living as a white guy troubled Warlock, the potential was too great to ignore. So what if they had tight asses, smaller dicks, and no rhythm when he could crush his enemies and rule the city right out in the open under the auspices of the law. He could literally get away with murder. And who said it had to be permanent? If those Voodoo niggas could make a muthafuckah switch bodies once, then they could probably do it again.

Demetrius' expression was skeptical.

"And how the hell are we supposed to do that?"

"You just let me worry about that. You worry about finding that fucking Cubano, Voodoo muthafuckah. Oh… and keep your phone close by. I'll call you when I can."

Warlock hung up the cell phone and shoved it between his collar and the meat of his burly neck. He turned and saw a homeless man lying nearby in a patch of overgrown weeds. The man was peeking out from under a large piece of cardboard. He was staring at him with glazed eyes bristling with disbelief. Warlock thought it strange that he hadn't noticed the man until now. Time froze as they stared at each other.

The homeless man looked away and evaluated his surroundings with trepidation. He peered through an opening in the thicket and saw the streets crowded with ugly. He saw ample bodies wrapped in tight clothing, soft bellies squeezing out from underneath child-sized shirts, dimpled, misshapen asses showing through light-colored stretchy pants, arm fat slapping air like fleshy rudders, a small mob of bastard children in tow. Drama queens hollered private conversations into cell phones with no shame, carrying on about trivial nonsense that spoke volumes about their sorry lives. They covered a medley of hood classics worthy of memorializing in a K-Tel Records compilation. The hits included:

"I don't need a man!"

"That bitch had the nerve to say…"

"That stank-ass hoe betta stay away from my man!"

"My baby-daddy ain't shit."

"God is the only man I serve."

"That nigga ain't got no money."

"Check Cashing Place Blues."

"Pin the Tail on the Baby Daddy"

"I'm not fat, I'm big-boned."

"General Tso's Chicken from the Ching Chong Stand."

"He hits me because he loves me."

"Hair did. Nails did. Bills come last."

He saw grown-ass men in days' old clothing eschewing work to loiter in the streets, laughing about the past and pontificating about all the ways the man is holding them down. He saw young thuglings practicing for lives filled with failure and regret and unnecessary violence. Peppered throughout the ugly parade were a few decent, hard-working folks sporting looks of grave disappointment.

The homeless man looked at the one-eyed goblin dog beast and asked groggily, "Am I dead? Is this Hell?"

"Yeah muthafuckah." Warlock calmly replied, "And I'm the devil. BOO!"

The homeless man screamed as if his life was ending. Warlock didn't want to disappoint him. He bared his saber-like fangs and stalked forward, saliva dripping from his jowls. The malformed canine monstrosity that Warlock's mind was trapped in, was hungry. It needed fuel. He could feel his flesh trying to repair itself. He certainly hoped that's what it was doing. His skin burned as if stricken with a fever. There was frenetic movement in the gaping wound where the creature's eye had been. The feeling was maddening, like a swarm of bees were buzzing around in his eye socket.

"Fuck! This shit is driving me crazy!" Warlock cried out.

"Get tha fuck away from me!" The old homeless man answered.

"Oh, shut the fuck up. I'm sure you've seen worse hallucinations than me."

"You're a hallucination?"

Every inch of Warlock's demon-spawned body rippled with activity as if the bee hive in his eye socket had moved into his flesh and bones. Even the latest bullet hole where he'd been shot by his dumb-ass nephew was itching and bubbling, the skin stretching, the surrounding muscles vibrating and undulating. He could feel his muscles, tendons, bones, and sinews shifting and reorganizing themselves. Whatever was happening to his body was excruciating and it was draining all of his strength. Instinctively, he knew that he needed energy, protein, to complete the process. The old raggedy-ass derelict with the Hefty bag full of aluminum cans, screaming like a girl and throwing fistfuls of garbage at him, looked like the perfect remedy for his hunger pangs. Warlock surged forward.

"Unfortunately for you, I'm real as fuck. Come here, muthafuckah!" He reached out for the old man and saw two hands that looked vaguely human, instead of just one. The newer, left, hand had thick black claws on the end of it. Warlock would have taken a moment to marvel at the new appendage, but the frenzied hunger that overtook him crowded all other thoughts from his mind.

The old man screamed again and Warlock clamped both hands on his throat and squeezed.

The man's esophagus gave little resistance in Warlock's

powerful hands. It was like pinching a Slurpee straw. The old derelict's face turned blue. His eyes bulged and his mouth opened wide, desperately trying to suck in oxygen. He attempted to fight Warlock off, punching at the tremendous canine with the big muscular arms and the suppurating wounds. There was a loud wet snap and the man's head dropped limply to the side. Blood dribbled out of his nose and mouth. Warlock's stomach growled.

Whatever was happening to him, it was not entirely bad. He opened his mouth wide and bit down on the man's face, crunching through bone as easily as if he were biting into one of his grandma's buttermilk biscuits. Half the man's skull crumbled into Warlock's mouth along with his face and a large portion of the man's grey matter. The taste was not unpleasant.

Man, this ain't bad at all. I could almost get used to this shit, Warlock thought. *If I could get pussy looking like this I'd consider riding this shit out. But I'm not down with looking like a damn dog for the rest of my life. I've got to get back in some man-skin.*

Warlock knelt down to continue his meal, punching into the old bum's stomach with his powerful arms, yanking out organs, and cramming them into his mouth. Heart, liver, kidneys, pancreas. He completely gutted him. Warlock could feel his strength returning in waves. He felt powerful, more powerful than he'd ever felt in his life. It was time to pay his old buddy Victor a visit. Warlock licked the blood and flecks of organ meat from his snout and smiled as he headed toward Center City and the police headquarters. If Victor wasn't there, he'd march right into City Hall if he had to but he was going to find that dago bastard and tear his soul out of his chest. The thought made him smile.

Victor Dom had been a thorn in Warlock's side for years. The overzealous fuck dragged him in for questioning every time anyone remotely involved in the drug trade turned up dead. It had made Warlock paranoid. He never used the same gun twice and always made sure to collect his shells and drill out the barrel of each gun before he discarded it. He always wore gloves, even in his own home, especially when handling a weapon or loading a clip. He hadn't touched a gun or a bullet with a bare hand in years. He vacuumed and scrubbed his vehicle incessantly and he used dogs, Demetrius's dogs, to dispose of any bodies he didn't want turning up. Whatever was left of the bodies when the dogs were done, he tossed into the crematorium at the local funeral parlor. Detective Victor Dom had never caught him doing so much as jaywalking. That didn't stop the man from trying and that made every job Warlock did more complicated. He never knew when he was under surveillance so he had to always assume that he was being watched.

Just to leave his house he would climb up to the roof, walk over a couple rooftops, and down the fire escape of the apartment building three doors down. He wasn't stupid enough to drive the Escalade on hits so he had an assortment of throwaway vehicles scattered throughout the neighborhood that he used and then discarded. All precautions made necessary by that piece-of-shit asshole Detective Dom. Soon, he would fix both problems.

That body belongs to me now, bitch. It's just a matter of time.

Then Warlock remembered who he'd sent to find the secret of his transference and felt his first moment of genuine doubt. His entire future was in the hands of a pot-smokin' dog breeder and some whacked-out Cuban speed-freak.

Could this night get any more fucked up?

A police car rounded the corner. It rolled slowly down the block, flashing a spotlight over the trees and shrubs and into the alleys. Someone must have called 911 when they heard the old bum's screams. Warlock's mind was already working, trying to figure out how to turn this to his advantage. He crept over to a nearby parked car and hid behind it, watching and waiting.

The spotlight landed on the old homeless man's gutted corpse and the squad car screeched to a halt and reversed. Warlock could hear the officers cursing loudly then the car doors opened and they stepped out of the vehicle. Their shoes slapped the asphalt loudly as they walked over to the sidewalk.

"Oh shit! Somebody tore this guy apart!"

They pulled their weapons and waved their flashlights around, looking for whoever was responsible for the carnage bleeding out onto the sidewalk. For a moment, Warlock was afraid they would spot him. He was looking less and less like a dog by the minute and more and more like… he didn't know what the fuck he looked like now. Some kind of demon or werewolf or something.

He could smell their sweat, the pepperoni pizza they'd both recently eaten, the cigarette the tall one smoked a few minutes before getting the call to respond to reports of a man screaming for his life.

"I'm calling it in."

Warlock slipped from behind the parked Ford Flex. There was no way he was going to let them call for backup.

"Who would do some shit like this?"

"I would." Warlock said as he closed the distance between the two officers faster than either of them could react. The first officer turned his gun toward the massive demon dog, with the human-like arms and hands, too slowly. Warlock relieved him of his handgun… and his hand. The second officer cried out in a half scream/half shout that sounded like something that would have come from a teenage girl. He fired two shots. One went high, sailing two feet over Warlock's head. The other went low, digging up chips of concrete at his feet. He didn't get a chance to fire a third time before Warlock barreled into him, shattered his kneecaps and brought him down hard. The officer's head struck the concrete and his eyes glazed. Calmly, Warlock crawled up his body and tore out his throat. The splash of hot blood in his mouth from the policeman's lacerated jugular and carotid arteries tasted wonderful as it washed down Warlock's throat. The other officer was screaming and holding his severed hand. The noise was attracting unwanted attention from the neighbors. Grudgingly, Warlock released his hold on the dead officer's throat and leapt on the policeman with the missing hand. With one swipe of his tremendous, muscle-bound arm he severed the man's head from his spine, abruptly silencing his screams.

Warlock allowed himself to feel a moment of satisfaction before he realized that he had accidently killed both officers, which left no one to drive him to the station. He looked down at his legs, which were still distinctly canine. There was no way he could drive himself. That meant he'd have to walk and the police station was a good sixteen blocks away. If he hurried and he was lucky, he might get there before the end of the midnight shift.

The big canine charged across the street and disappeared into the nearest alley. He would have to stay off the street as much as possible. The only people he'd run into in the alleys were the homeless, gangs, crackheads, junkies, and prostitutes with their tricks. None of them were likely to call the cops even if they saw a blood-soaked gargoyle running through an alley. And the Philadelphia PD weren't likely to believe any of them if they did.

Warlock hadn't run more than four blocks before the night erupted with the sound of police sirens. Cops were everywhere. Even the alleys weren't safe. Police officers were rounding up the crackheads, winos and junkies for questioning.

"Shit!" Warlock growled. "I need to get my ugly ass off the street."

He scanned the street for someplace to hide then smiled when he saw the sign on the small brownstone at the end of the block, *The Harriet Tubman Home for Abused Women*. Perhaps this was going to be a good night after all. A home full of helpless-ass women would make the perfect place to hide out until the streets cooled off.

***

"This is bullshit!" Demetrius shouted, punching the steering wheel.

How the fuck did I get into this mess? Why does this bullshit always happen to me?

He had no idea how in the hell he was supposed to get Salvador and his merry band of mischief makers to agree to transfer Warlock's body into some other fool. He didn't even know if that shit could be done. But given all the madness he'd seen in the last 24 hours, he was inclined to believe it was possible.

Demetrius pulled the Cadillac up in front of Salvadore's house. For once, the place was silent. He still didn't know how he was going to convince the man or his family to fix Warlock. He hunted around in the Escalade, looking for a gun or a rifle or something but the ride was clean.

Shit! How the fuck is a damn hitman not going to have a gun in his ride?

There was not so much as a knife in the glove box or under the seats. Coercing the crazy bastard into helping was definitely out of the question. That meant he had to somehow talk him into it. He didn't know what he possibly had to bargain with.

Demetrius let out a deep sigh and climbed out of the Escalade. His heart was pounding in his chest and his stomach felt jittery. If he fucked this up he was certain that Warlock would kill him and now it wouldn't be quick and clean. No bullet through the brain. He'd rip him apart with those big-ass teeth of his.

I am so fucked.

He knocked on the door. No one answered. He knocked again, harder, then he rang the doorbell. The door jerked open and Salvador staggered into the doorway looking drowsy, unshaven, unwashed, and worst of all sober. Sober Salvador was irritable, intolerant, and easily provoked. Demetrius was hoping for high-as-fuck Salvador, who was much easier to deal with.

"What the fuck do you want, Meech? Why the fuck are you knockin' on my damn door in the middle of the fuckin' night?"

Demetrius didn't know what to say. Everything just seemed so unreal. He opened his mouth and nothing came out.

"It's too fuckin' late to be fuckin' around, Meech. I'm not taking that damn dog back. Just stay the fuck away from us." Salvador turned to leave and Demetrius reached out and grabbed his arm.

Salvador turned quickly, faster than Demetrius would have ever thought the guy capable of. Before he knew what happened, Salvador had pulled a long knife that looked like a ceremonial dagger, like something from one of those old Conan movies, and placed it against Demetrius's throat.

"Don't you ever put your hands on me, muthafucka! You hear me? I'll slit your fucking throat you ever touch me again!"

"Yo, man! Chill! Stop trippin'! I didn't mean shit. I just need to talk to you, Yo."

Salvador pulled the knife away and Demetrius rubbed his throat.

"Then speak, nigga! What you want?"

Demetrius was still rubbing his throat.

"My dog... the little demon muthefucka that Sheba gave birth to..."

Salvador smiled. The expression seemed to bleed all of the warmth from the air.

"Yeah? What about the muthafucka?"

"There's something wrong with that thing. It killed a bunch of people and now it's got somebody else's soul inside of it. It's like possessed or some shit."

Salvador was still smiling. He leaned against the doorway and lit up a blunt, a fat cigar filled with marijuana. Demetrius's eyes zeroed in on it and his mouth watered. He wanted to get high so badly he didn't know what to do with himself.

"Can I get a hit off that?"

Salvador's reptilian smile widened. His eyes were black and filled with shadows as if he had no soul at all.

"You sure?" He asked, holding out the blunt.

Demetrius didn't want to get high that bad. Who knew what kind of shit this crazy muthafucka was smoking.

"Naw... uh... nevernmind."

47

"So why you commin' here with this bullshit?"

"You gotta help me!"

Salvador pointed the knife right between Demetrius's eyes.

"I ain't gotta do shit but eat, shit, and die."

"Look. I can't make you do shit. But the nigga who's inside that damn demon dog you muthafuckas made is Warlock. You know who Warlock is?"

Salvador nodded slowly. His mouth had fallen open and his eyes were wide. He looked terrified.

"If I don't find a way to get him into a new body he's going to kill us both."

"Shit! Fuck, man. How tha fuck did this shit happen? Warlock? Fuck, man!"

"Yeah. You see what I'm sayin'? We're both fucked if we don't do somethin'."

"Why the fuck did you tell him I was involved?" Salavdor asked in a near panic.

"Cause you are, muthafucka! You fools created the damn thing! You killed my fuckin' dog makin' that fuckin' monster!"

"Okay, okay. Just shut the fuck up. Where is he? I'll go wake grandma and we'll get it all straightened out."

"Um… he ain't here."

"Well, where tha fuck is he?"

"He's out gettin' a body for you to transfer him into. I'm supposed to wait for his call and then pick them both up. He wanted me to bring you to him."

"I can't do the shit by myself. My grandma is the one with all the power."

"Then wake tha bitch up and bring her ass too!"

"Don't ever call my grandma a bitch, negrito!" Salvador stopped and said.

"Sorry."

***

Warlock stalked around the back of the building, ripped through a chain link fence, and made his way across the yard, hugging tight to the shadows. There were security lights all around the building, illuminating the backyard, the alley, and the front of the building. There was no way to approach without being seen. He had to hope that everyone inside was already asleep.

I hope these bitches are fine, Warlock thought. He wasn't into rape. Rapists were all a bunch of bitch-made cowards. Besides, sex was only good if the hoes wanted it. Still, he didn't relish the idea of being holed up with a bunch of ugly bitches. If he had to wait the cops out, he at least wanted some nice tits and asses to look at while he did it.

He made his way across the lawn and crept up the stairs to the back porch. The door was locked as he knew it would be. You'd have to be a fool to leave your door unlocked in any neighborhood in this town. Even in Chestnut Hill they locked their doors. He tried a couple windows. They were locked tight. The sound of sirens filled the night in all directions like the cries of tortured animals. Police officers, in squad cars and on foot, patrolled the streets and alleyways. They were searching for a cop killer and the city was sparing no expense. A lot of overtime was being paid to hunt down the man who butchered two Philly PD officers. No one on the police force was going to sleep tonight. Not until they found him. But Warlock had no intention of being found. He didn't care how many more bodies he had to destroy. No one was taking him alive and he wasn't yet ready to die.

Warlock stared at the door, trying to puzzle his way through this dilemma. If he made too much noise someone might hear him and call the police. With the cops all over the streets they might even hear him. Still, staying out in the open was not an option. If he stayed out there too long the cops were bound to spot him. And it wouldn't be too hard for them to connect him with the death of their fellow officers. A blood-spattered two hundred pound bullmastiff with a face like a gargoyle and arms like a weightlifter was not going to be hard to pick out of a line-up. At least if they found him while he was in the women's shelter he'd have hostages. Warlock walked around the side of the house and tried a couple more windows. They were all locked.

I guess I'm gonna have to make some noise, Warlock thought before he smashed through the back door, reducing it to kindling. He was in a large kitchen. The lights were out but he could make out most of the room's features clearly. Glass crunched under his fists and paws as he made his way out of the kitchen and into a large dining area with two long tables. Beyond it was a long hallway.

A startled scream came from somewhere above.

"What the fuck was that?" The voice sounded young. Playful and lilting. A child's voice or a young adult.

"Sylvia? Is that you down there, girl?" This one was much older. Raspy. The voice of a grandmother or great grandmother.

"It ain't me. I'm right here!" another voice answered. An adult voice but not too old. A woman in her thirties or forties perhaps.

"Who's down there? I'm calling the police!" The older voice shouted but there was no sound of footsteps. She was hesitating, waiting for a reply. Scared.

"I'm going to see what the hell that was." Said the younger woman.

"Be careful, Missy." Someone whispered.

"Don't worry, I've got my baseball bat."

"What about that shotgun?"

"Girl, ain't no bullets in that old thing."

"I'm coming with you." the old woman said.

"Should we call da police?" another voice asked. A hoodrat. Probably some crackwhore.

"Wait. It might not be anything," the old woman replied. It was clear from the authoritative tone of her voice and the respect in the voices of the other women that she ran the place. Warlock tried to decide whether it would be better to take her out or keep her alive and use her to control the other women. He might be able to tie them up and force one of them to drive him the fuck out of there, past the police. One of these bitches had to have a vehicle.

Several other doors opened and Warlock heard more voices. He tried to count each new voice. Thirteen. Fourteen maybe. More than he expected. It would be hard to control them all and what if they had cell phones? One of them might already be calling the cops. He needed to neutralize them quickly.

Footsteps crept down the stairs. Warlock moved in the direction of the footsteps. A light went on at the end of the hallway. If someone stepped into the hallway they would spot him immediately. He started running, closing the distance between himself and the women.

"Oh shit! Oh shit!"

"What? What?"

"You hear that? Something's coming right at us!"

Another light came on in the hallway, temporarily blinding Warlock. He kept running blind.

"Ahhhh! Aaaaaiiiihhhh!"

"What the fuck is that thing!"

The old woman was not quite as old as Warlock had imagined. Short graying hair, wide hips, thick thighs, breasts the size of small turkeys perched atop a bloated belly. She looked like his older sister.

Turkey Breasts froze on the bottom step. Warlock stopped running. The other women were packed on the staircase a few feet behind Turkey Breasts screaming and bitching at each other as they fought for space in the small area.

The hallway was long. The stairs at the far end ran perpendicular to it. Fifteen feet of hallway stood between them, far enough that Turkey Breasts squinted and tilted her head from one side to the other to validate what she saw standing there staring back at her.

Warlock was getting used to the look that twisted the older woman's ugly face. It was a peculiar mixture of shock and horror wrapped in utter mindfuck.

"That's right, bitch. Take it all in." He crept forward and

held his hands up one-by-one and showed them to her. He twisted and turned them so that there was no mistaking that they were human. "It don't make a lick-a-sense, does it? That's because this is all just a dream. Now just close your eyes and—"

"Sweet G-ZUS!" Turkey Breasts words jumped out like a sneeze. She turned and started to run back up the stairs. She spread her arms and flapped them at the small jumble of emotionally damaged women packed on the staircase.

"GO! GO! GO!"

The women screamed and ran up the stairs. Turkey Breasts ran behind them moving like someone to whom rigorous physical activity was a foreign concept. Her wide ass was round and lumpy and it seemed to take up two thirds of her back. Her ample cheeks jiggled and separated like bags of wet mud fully packed.

"Shit!" Warlock yelled and ran toward the staircase. He would need to turn on a dime to transition from the floor to the staircase and climb the steps without stopping. It wouldn't be an easy feat considering his strange mixture of limbs. He tried anyway.

Warlock's hands and feet slid out from under him. His massive bulk hit the floor sideways and slid into the wall with a thump and rattled the entire first floor. He kept his eyes trained on the top of the staircase as he slid and saw the old woman's wide, fat ass disappear down a hallway on the second floor.

The women were screaming at the top of their lungs. The hoodrat was yelling, "Dey shoot-in'! Dey shoot-in'!"

"What was it?! What did you see?!" A young woman yelled over her shoulder at Turkey Breasts.

"Just go! Keep going!" Turkey Breasts replied.

Warlock heard several doors slam shut on the second floor. The screaming died down a notch with each slammed door until finally the house was nearly silent.

Warlock shook off a twinge of lightheadedness, and then scrambled to his feet and ran up the stairs.

Standing motionless and alert at the top of the stairs,

Warlock stared down a long hallway with several doors on either side. All of the doors were closed. He heard movement and whispering coming from some of the rooms.

He tilted his short, thick muzzle upward and sniffed the air. His sense of smell had become so acute that he could smell fear. In this case it was laced with the pungent aroma of menstrual blood. That kind of thing usually made Warlock's stomach turn, but at the moment he didn't seem to mind. In fact, he found the collective fragrance intoxicating as it wafted out from under a few of the doors. His eyes fluttered. He began to salivate.

Warlock heard Turkey Breast's voice coming from the room two doors down on the left side—Room 3B. He aimed his ear at the door marked 3B. His hearing had improved as well, though to a lesser degree than his sense of smell.

Even though she was whispering, Turkey Breast's voice hit him loud and clear. It sounded like she was standing right next to him, whispering in his ear.

"I don't know what it was," she whispered to someone.

"Whadayou mean, you don't know? You saw it didn't you?"

"It looked like a dog," whispered another woman. "A big, ugly-ass thing."

"Wasn't like no dog I ever seen," Turkey Breasts challenged.

"Then what was it? One-a-yer *demons*?"

A pause.

"Oh you can't be serious."

"Hey! You don't talk to Ms. Dorothy like that."

"I'll talk to her however I damn well—"

"Would you guys cut it out!" whispered a female voice Warlock hadn't heard before.

Damn! How many chicks they got up in this place?!

He had stopped counting at around 15. He made a mental note.

Turkey breasts = Ms. Dorothy.

"Now listen…" said the new voice. "It's probly just somebody's dog that got loose. You know how these ignantass fools around here are with their Rotties and their Pits."

"But I… I h… heard it talk," said Ms. Dorothy.

"What?!!!!!"

"I heard it too"; a man's voice. "Ya'll didn't hear it?"

"I couldn't hear anything over all the screaming."

"Me neither."

"Nope."

"Dem talkin' dogs ain't no joke," the hoodrat warned in a dumb accent. "Dey be makin' people do all kinna things."

"Quadeira!" The new girl scolded.

"I'm serious! Like that dog that told Sam I aim to kill all dem people up in New York."

"That was Son of Sam. And he was crazy. Now, *SHHHHH!*"

Hoodrat = Quadeira.

The room got quiet as the women, save for Ms. Dorothy, and maybe Quadeira, reached essentially the same conclusion—there was a big, ugly dog loose in the house. It belonged to a crazy man who meant to use it as a weapon to lure them out and most likely rape them.

Warlock could hear similar whispered conversations coming from some of the other rooms, but he kept his focus on 3B.

"We gotta call the police!"

"How? All our cell phones is in Ms. Dorothy's room way at the end-a-tha hall?"

"You and your damn curfew!"

"Hey! I said don't talk to her like that!"

"It's for your own good," said Ms. Dorothy sounding shaken by the image of a talking goblin dog thing that refused to get out of her mind.

"Lotta good it's gonna do us now."

"*SHHHH!*" The new girl hissed. "You hear that?"

She was talking about the terrible ruckus coming from Ms. Dorothy's room.

Warlock tore through the room at the end of the hall looking for the confiscated cell phones. He came to an end table next to the bed that he had just flipped on its side. The phones were in the bottom drawer 20 or 30 of them.

Warlock slid a pillowcase from one of the pillows on the floor. He scooped up phones in handfuls and dropped them in the pillowcase. He choked the open end in both hands and swung the pillowcase like a baseball bat, against the floor until he was satisfied that the cellphones were unusable. Then he remembered the phone stuffed in his collar. He reached up and felt around the area. The cellphone was gone.

"Shit!" he groaned. Now he needed a phone. He could've used one of the phones in the bag. *Nice move, genius.*

He heard a door creak open out in the hallway. It was the door marked 3B. The goblin dog sunk low to the ground and skulked toward the door, ready to pounce on whoever was stupid enough to come out into the hallway. He hoped it wasn't Ms. Dorothy. His plan was still to use her to control the other women. However, the aroma of fear and menstrual blood was stronger than ever now and it had him fiendin' to sink his fangs into soft, warm flesh; to taste the first rush of blood, and to hear the crunch of bone.

Warlock was so focused on 3B that he didn't see Missy tiptoe out of a room that he had already crawled past. She was wielding a baseball bat in both hands. Her face was fixed in a savage grimace. She choked up on the bat's skinny neck as she sneaked up behind the goblin dog. Her eyes widened as she raised the bat over her head.

Warlock heard a noise behind him. He whipped around and…

***

"So we're supposed to just drive around until he calls?" Salvador impatiently asked.

Judging by his tone of voice, Salvador wasn't pleased with the idea, which made Demetrius reluctant to answer him. Demetrius was getting tired of chauffeuring people around. He was tired of driving, period. And he didn't trust these Cubanos one bit, especially the old woman seated in the passenger seat staring at the side of his head as he drove.

She had beady eyes recessed so far back into her face that the surrounding, wrinkled skin looked like fleshy blinders. The oval pits were heavily shadowed, which made them appear hollow. He wanted to tell her to back the fuck up off of him, but Salvador would probably view that as disrespect and he struck Demetrius as the type who would overreact to something like that.

"That's what he said," Demetrius replied.

Occasionally Salvador would speak to the old woman in Spanish.

"Hope you guys aren't talking about me," Demetrius joked.

Salvador smiled and said, "Of course not."

The old woman kept looking at him with those beady eyes. It was really beginning to make him feel uncomfortable. First of all, he had seen the kind of freaky, hardcore violence they were capable of. Murder was a young man's game as far Demetrius was concerned. That this old woman seemed okay with it, made her seem even more cold and inaccessible than those beady eyes made her look. That the violence had a religious component made it worse.

"Umm… seriously. What were you guys talking about if you don't mind me asking?"

"Don't worry about it." Said Salvador.

Shit, man. These crazy bastards are up to something.

Demetrius drove around in circles feeling pressured by the old woman's unyielding gaze.

"Hey man. I don't think your grandmother likes me too much," he remarked to Salvador.

"She don't like nobody she don't know."

"Fair enough."

He drove around a while longer. The side of his face was starting to itch where the old woman's hollow oval pits were aimed. He felt that if he didn't say something to make her stop he was going to react in a way that would lead to unnecessary drama.

"Can you tell your grandmother something for me?" he said to Salvador.

"Tell her yourself."

"I thought she didn't speak any English."

"She doesn't."

"Oh. But she can understand it, though?"

"Not a word."

Demetrius rolled his eyes and exhaled, frustrated.

"So, how the hell is she supposed to—"

"She understands people, acere. Try her. You'll see."

Demetrius waited until they stopped at a red light and then he turned to the old woman and immediately squinted at the palpable heat radiating from her beady-eyed gaze. It was like looking into the sun.

"Look. No offense, but in the future I think it's best that you get your dogs from someone else." He said.

The old woman didn't respond and for a moment they were locked in a stare down. Salvador was smiling in the back seat like he was in on a joke that Demetrius was the butt of.

A car horn blared and startled Demetrius. He looked and saw that the light had turned green.

Crazy fucking bastards, Demetrius thought as he stepped on the gas.

***

The women stood around Warlock's unconscious husk wondering what sort of abomination he was. They ultimately decided to put the goblin dog thing that must have been sent by the devil in the closet in room 3B.

Warlock awoke with a splitting headache as two women dragged him by the legs. When his head cleared and he realized what had happened, he swung his claws at the nearest thing, which happened to be Ms. Dorothy's bloated, low-hanging belly. He moved so quickly and his claws were so sharp that in the chaos of the moment, no one, including Ms. Dorothy, realized what had happened until they got Warlock into the closet, slammed the door shut, and wedged a high-backed wooden chair under the doorknob.

Warlock banged on the door from the other side. The doorframe rattled. The wooden chair was leaning on its rear legs, which kept inching forward as he pounded the door with both fists. Sylvia, who was standing closest to it, repositioned the chair after each blow.

There were seven women in the room. A few more had just run in from the hall.

Somebody screamed.

"OH MY GOD! MS. DOROTHY!

Ms. Dorothy staggered backward on wobbly legs. Her face was curiously arranged as she placed her hand underneath her bloated, low-hanging belly and lifted it so that she could see what was causing the sudden burning, throbbing sensation. Blood poured through her fingers and over her hand and wrist, gushing faster as she lifted. A plump, partially severed tentacle pushed out and slapped the rapidly expanding puddle on the floor beneath her. The other end reached into the enormous wound in her gut that opened like a mouth slobbering out half-chewed food.

Ms. Dorothy looked up at the ceiling with pleading eyes.

"Please Lord," she muttered just before she fainted and her soft, unruly girth toppled backward and hit the floor hard.

"Open this fucking door!" Warlock repeatedly demanded as he continued to pound the door with his fists.

The screaming women split into two factions. One ran over to help Sylvia with the closet door while the other one crowded around Ms. Dorothy, who lay dying on her back.

"Somebody call an ambulance," one of the women yelled.

"The cellphones!" Yelled another one as she took off running toward Ms. Dorothy's room.

"Tell her to hurry!" Sylvia screamed over her shoulder. "I don't know how long this chair's gonna hold."

"You bitches shoulda killed me when you had the chance!" Warlock growled in a half-human voice. "Cause I swear, I'm gonna rip you all to shreds when I get outta here! Every last one-a-you bitches!"

A woman who looked too healthy to be a resident of

the Harriet Tubman Home searched through Ms. Dorothy's ransacked room. She had found the pillowcase full of broken cellphones right away and tried one after the other until she came to one that still worked.

"Here. Use this one!" she said as she tossed the phone to Missy who was waiting in the hallway. And then she started searching for Ms. Dorothy's keys.

The Harriet Tubman Home was a halfway house for abused women, many of whom were also alcoholics and drug addicts. The place was put on lockdown every night at 10pm to keep the alcoholics and addicts from trying to sneak out, and to keep the abusive husbands, boyfriends, and former pimps from trying to sneak in. The reinforced Plexiglass windows and the heavy, steel security doors at the front and back entrance were all barred and alarmed. Ms. Dorothy had the keys to the doors hidden somewhere in her room. She had been warned many times that her lockdown procedure presented a fire safety risk.

"My girls require extreme measures," was her response. "If the law has a problem with it, then let them put it in writing. That way they can be responsible for what happens to these girls as a result. Until then lockdown stays as is."

"I can't find the keys!" The healthy-looking woman yelled back. Her voice sounded desperate, near panic.

Missy was on the phone with the 911 Dispatcher. The reception was bad, so she had to keep asking, "Can you hear me now?"

"OH MY GOD. I THINK SHE'S DYING!" Cried a voice from 3B.

"We need an ambulance! And the police! Fast!" Missy demanded.

Warlock pounded and growled, "YOU'RE DEAD! ALLA YOU ARE FUCKING DEAD!"

"We're at the Harriet Tubman on Wallace. Please hurry! There's a... *thing*... some kinda dog in here! He hurt Ms. Dorothy really bad! I don't know if she's gonna make it."

"Some kind of dog?" The nasally dispatcher queried.

"Yes. We have it trapped in the closet, but I don't know

how long we can keep him there."

"YOU HAVE TO STAY WITH US, MS. DOROTHY!" Came the voice from 3B. "YOU HAVE TO STAY AWAKE!"

"Please hurry!" Missy pleaded into the phone.

Warlock growled and pounded.

"What kind of dog?" asked the dispatcher. She spoke with a calm demeanor that contradicted the chaos unraveling on the second floor of the Harriet Tubman Home. It came across as cold and unsympathetic to Missy, exacerbating her growing sense of helplessness.

"I don't know!" She whined, annoyed with the dispatcher's questions. "It had arms like a damn man. And it talked!"

The dispatcher paused.

"Excuse me, but did you say—"

"Yes Goddammit! Just send them! Please! We don't have much time!"

"MS. DOROTHY! MS. DOROTHY! NO!"

The healthy-looking woman continued to search Ms. Dorothy's room.

Missy hung up the cellphone and ran into 3B fearing that Ms. Dorothy had expired.

A huddle of women knelt and crouched around Ms. Dorothy, whimpering and sobbing. They seemed indifferent to the vast puddle of blood that dampened their knees and feet. Quadeira, the hoodrat was among them.

"Is sh… she…?" Missy asked.

"Don't even say it!" scolded the woman who knelt by Ms. Dorothy's head holding her face in both hands. She shook Ms. Dorothy's head from side to side and yelled, "Please, Ms. Dorothy! You have to wake up! The ambulance is on its way!"

"You can't die, Ms. Dorothy! We need you!"

"Just try to hang on a lil bit longer!"

"Don't go inta the light, Carol-Anne!" Quadeira added. "Stay away from the light."

The other women shifted incredulously. If they hadn't known Quadeira the way they did—that her brain was fried to shit from years of smoking crack—they might have thought she was making light of the situation. Unfortunately, she was dead serious.

Sylvia, and the other woman by the closet door, had stopped to focus on Ms. Dorothy. At some point Sylvia realized that Warlock had stopped pounding and making threats.

"Hey! Listen!" she whispered and pointed at the closet door. The pounding and the threats had been replaced by stretching and tearing and crackling sounds. The thing inside was breathing erratically and groaning in pain.

"What's happening in there?" Someone asked.

I dunno, Sylvia shrugged.

They listened until the noise suddenly stopped. A few moments passed. And then, out of the blue, a wheezing build-up turned to giddy laughter. There were hints of maniacal satisfaction and glee in the timbre and pitch of the laughter coming from inside the closet.

Sylvia backed away from the door. The other women moved in tandem with her.

The laughter grew more intense. And then it stopped as suddenly as the pounding and the threats had a few minutes earlier.

There was silence, and then…

The closet door swelled and split before exploding outward in a hail of splinters and debris. Sylvia stumbled backward and ducked out of the way of the chair that flew by over her head and crashed into a nearby wall. Wood chunks and splinters rained at the screaming, cowering women.

Sylvia tripped over her own feet. She fell and immediately rolled onto her back to see what had caused the explosion. A number of the women ran screaming out of the room.

Standing fully upright in front of the closet, a mastiff-headed, man-thing glared at the frightened women who remained in the room. The beast stood almost seven feet with floppy ears, huge jaws with tusk-like fangs, and eyes that swirled with hate. Its body was covered in short, matted black fur. Long, heavily-muscled arms tipped with claws hung from a barrel-chested canine torso perched atop one fully developed human leg and one that was human down to the knee. The rest of the limb resembled a dog's hind leg. Between his legs, his penis was now covered in a hairy foreskin which sheathed a narrow organ that looked like an infected sea slug. The transformation had healed Warlock's wounds and mostly corrected the ugly imperfections in the marriage of dog and man. Now, he looked like a true, bipedal mixture of human and Bull Mastif.

Warlock felt invigorated, like he could take on the world. His chest heaved from the rush of adrenaline. He spread his powerful; arms and let out a deep, passionate roar. A spit bubble burst in his mouth and the twisty, stringy remnants rode the wind from his hot breath. He suddenly became light-headed. He staggered briefly and checked his balance. His sight was replaced by an abrupt vision of rampaging beasts that were spitting images of the monstrosity he'd become sans the battle scars.

The women's screaming intensified as the room cleared out. The shrill sound pierced through Warlock's mind. He saw Sylvia resting on her arms, half-sitting and half lying down on the floor, her eyes filled with horrified awe.

Warlock approached her. A dull thump announced every footfall.

"Looks like your friends left you," Warlock taunted. His voice rolled out differently, like an animal attempting to speak as a man. It made his words difficult to understand. "Don't worry. They're gonna get their's too."

He raised his clawed hand…

A horrible noise leapt out of the ether. It was coming from behind the dresser on the other side of the room—a cellphone ringtone set to "Superman" by Soulja Boy.

> *Soulja Boy up In it (oh)*
> *Watch Me Crank It*
> *Watch Me Roll*
> *Watch Me Crank Dat Soulja Boy*
> *den Super Man Dat (oh)*

Now watch me yuuuuuuuuh
(Crank Dat Soulja Boy)
Now watch me yuuuuuuuuh
(Crank Dat Soulja Boy)
Now watch me Yuuuuuuuuh
(Crank Dat Soulja Boy)
Now watch me Yuuuuuuuuh
(Crank Dat Soulja Boy)

Warlock slapped his hands over his ears, threw his head back, and cried out in pain. It was the worst fucking thing he'd ever heard. He loped over to the dresser. His legs still felt awkward and ungainly and he nearly lost his balance crossing the room. He shoved the dresser aside. Missy was crouched behind it trying desperately to stop the ringtone from playing. If she hadn't been so scared, she might've realized that it was as easy as pressing "Ignore."

She froze and turned her head slowly, reluctantly, and looked sheepishly up at Warlock. Sensing her doom, she started crying. She looked away sobbing, reached out her arm and offered the cellphone to the angry beast.

Warlock roared at her and then snatched the cellphone from Missy's hand and smacked her into the wall. Her bones shattered like glass on impact and she crumbled lifelessly to the floor.

Warlock looked down at his hand. He was holding Missy's severed arm. Her hand was still clutching the cellphone. The ringtone continued to sound.

Warlock cocked his arm back and hurled the severed arm with the cellphone clutched in a death grasp at the floor as hard as he could. And then he stomped on it until only small pieces remained.

Police sirens jumped at him from outside the window. Red and blue light set the room aglow like a nightclub that catered to violent fetishes. Tires screeched out in the street. Doors opened and slammed shut. Hard soles smacked the pavement. The women were downstairs pounding on the Plexiglass windows and screaming bloody murder.

Warlock hurried over to the window and looked out. The street was crowded with police cars hastily parked.

***

"So, I said to the guy, 'Speedy Gonzales was Mexican, you stupid sapingo!' Then I shot him in the kneecaps and cut out his tongue just for saying that racist shit."

Of the three stories Salvador had told Demetrius over the past hour, that one was the tamest in terms of violent content. He was starting to think that maybe it was time for a complete life change.

The old Cuban woman had finally stopped staring at him and was looking out the window and commenting under her breath in Spanish about everything she saw. Suddenly, she bucked in her seat as if to a prolonged surge of electricity. Her face tightened. Her teeth clenched. She arched her back painfully and clutched the armrests.

Startled, Demetrius leaned away from the old woman.

"Qué le dicen las visiones?" [What are the visions telling you?] Salvador leaned forward and asked her. He didn't seem all that worried by what was happening.

The woman's rigid posture loosened. She relaxed into her seat taking deep breaths. And then she turned to Salvador and said, "Lo vi!" [I saw him!]

"Who? Warlock?"

"Sí! Tenemos que apresurarnos! Debemos pararlo antes de que la transformación sea completa!" [Yes! We have to hurry! We must stop him before the transformation is complete!]

"Shit! Where is he?"

"Una casa en Calle Wallace! Harriet Tubman!" [A house on Wallace Street! The Harriet Tubman!]

"Ahhhh. If it's not too much to ask, I'd like to know what the hell is going on?" Demetrius asked.

"Get to the Harriet Tubman Home! Fast!" Salvador replied.

"But I'm supposed to wait for—"

"Just go! Now! Trust me on this, acere!"

Demetrius stepped on the gas.

"No! Espere!" [No! Wait!] the old woman yelled. And then she turned her ear toward the sound of an approaching siren.

A moment later an ambulance appeared at the mouth of a small street that ran perpendicular to where they were on Broad. The old woman extended her arm and pointed a finger toward Demetrius' feet.

"Hey! What the fuck!" Demetrius yelled as the steering wheel yanked sideways and the SUV sped up. They were heading straight for the speeding ambulance as it crossed Broad Street.

Demetrius grabbed the wheel and struggled to turn the SUV away, but the wheel wouldn't budge. He frantically pumped the brakes to no avail.

The ambulance veered sideways to avoid the SUV. The SUV's brakes locked and brought them to a dead stop right in front of it. The ambulance skidded to a stop inches from the SUV. The sirens were still blaring. Lights flashing.

The two paramedics jumped out yelling.

"Are you out of your fucking mind!"

"You're supposed to yield, Goddammit! Can't you hear the fucking siren?!"

The old woman slid Salvador a knowing glance as she calmly exited the SUV and walked around to the front. Salvador got out after her and stood back.

"What are you doing?!" yelled paramedic #1. "Get back in your vehicle and move that damn thing out of—"

The man stopped suddenly and looked down at himself. His eyes widened.

"Holy Shit!" He yelled and started swatting himself all over. "Get 'em offa me! Get 'em offa me!"

The old woman grinned and shifted her focus to paramedic #2. Her eyes squinted with recognition.

Paramedic #1 ran around in circles screaming "Get 'em offa me!" and swatting at himself.

"What? What's wrong?!" Paramedic #2 yelled at his

colleague, dumbfounded. And then he turned to the old woman and demanded, "What, the hell, did you do to him, you crazy bitch?!"

Salvador flashed a hateful look at Paramedic #2. With his fists balled, he took a step toward the man.

The old woman gave Salvador a look that said, "I got this." Salvador backed off and smiled knowingly.

Demetrius sat in the back of the ambulance as it raced toward Wallace Street where the Harriet Tubman Home was located. Salvador was driving with his grandmother in the passenger seat, squeezed into a paramedic's uniform that was way too small. Demetrius was looking out the rear window as he arched and slinked into the second paramedic's uniform. In the distance he saw two paramedics stripped down to their underwear.

Paramedic #1 was still running around swatting at invisible insects that covered his body and screaming, "Get 'em offa me!"

Paramedic #2 was staggering down Green Street punching, and choking, and clawing himself. At one point the man grabbed a clutch of his own hair and slammed his face into the hood of a parked car until it was horribly disfigured and covered in blood.

Fuck, man! Demetrius lamented. *Remind me never to cross these twisted muthafuckahs.*

Along the way the old woman had another vision that told her that Detective Victor Dom was at the scene, and that he had already formulated a plan to enter the building along with the paramedics, disguised as one of them.

She instructed Demetrius via Salvador to turn over his uniform to the detective when he asked.

The ambulance arrived at the jumble of squad cars in front of the Harriet Tubman Home. All the flashing lights made Salvador nervous. He snatched a wool cap from his back pocket and pulled it down to his eyebrows to conceal his tattoos, and then he turned off the engine and sat back in his seat and tried to act like an ambulance driver. The old woman climbed out of the vehicle to a sea of quizzical reactions to her ill-fitting uniform.

Demetrius hopped out the back of the ambulance and joined the old woman just as Victor Dom hurried over to them. The detective made a face at the old woman's outfit, but then it was right to business.

"You got an extra uniform in there?" He pointed to the van and asked the old woman. "I'm goin' in with you."

"You can take his uniform," she replied.

Demetrius was slow in realizing that she was talking about his uniform. He had seen how the words that poured from her mouth were slightly out of sync with the movement of her lips. And her voice sounded different. Based on the way her mouth moved, he could tell that she was speaking in Spanish. But the voice that came out spoke the words in unaccented English.

"What did you say?" asked Demetrius.

The old woman smiled.

"I said—"

"Nevermind!" Victor shouted. "Where's that uniform?"

Demetrius shrugged out of his uniform and handed the top to the detective.

"You're going in there?"

The detective looked at him and smiled smugly.

"Somebody has to and that's what the taxpayers pay me for."

Demetrius chuckled and shook his head.

"A real hero, huh?"

He wondered how heroic the cop would feel when he saw Warlock coming at him. He'd probably piss himself before he got his guts ripped out.

The detective ignored him.

"Give me a medical bag or something to carry in with me."

Demetrius looked around for a medical bag of some kind to give to the detective. He couldn't find anything.

"Come on! Just give me anything!"

Finally, Demetrius located an orange bag that looked like it held medical supplies and handed it to the detective.

The detective placed his gun and badge inside it and raced toward the line of police vehicles with Salvadore's Grandma in tow.

"Fuck. This is going to end badly." Demetrius whispered to himself.

***

Warlock's mind was filled with violence. He had always been a cold calculating killer. He delighted in the fear his reputation inspired. He even loved the fear in his victim's eyes, but the very act of killing had never affected him one way or the other. He wasn't one of those freaks who got off on bloodshed. Not like a serial killer. But now, his mind was filled with thoughts of carnage, the smell of the young women's flesh was maddening and their screams were arousing more than just his curiosity.

Ever since he'd found his soul imprisoned within the flesh of this demon-dog, he'd feared that it would begin to affect his mind. He wondered what had happened to the demon's soul. Now, he had his answer. It had merged with his own. He hadn't been aware of it before. He'd been too busy trying to find a way out of his predicament. But now he could see the beast's thoughts, feel its desires, and they were horrible. Blood-soaked images flashed through Warlock's mind of body parts dismembered, organs torn out and devoured, bones crushed. Warlock recognized some of the faces of the gangbangers and mafia capos the beast had torn apart at Warlock's urging, memories of what he'd done to them. Some of the others were the women in the shelter, the creature's desires. But the visions went far beyond that.

In his mind, Warlock could see an endless swath of broken humanity, ripped apart, raped and devoured. If the beast had its way, the violence would never end. Warlock noted it as a simple fact, a mere curiosity. He didn't approve or disapprove of the dog-thing's intentions. He had no genuine love of humanity. People were simply a means to an end. Warlock could not care less if the beast killed a million of his fellow men, as long as he wasn't inside the thing when it happened. If the creature wanted to kill, that was its business. Warlock didn't give a fuck. He was going to get out of this hell-spawned thing and into a normal human body then put as much distance between this creature and himself as humanly possible. If he'd had any thoughts of staying in his current situation, seeing the demon's thoughts had settled that. No matter how powerful, how invincible he felt, it wasn't worth his humanity or his sanity.

As a precaution, he probed the demon's mind for a weakness, something he could use to destroy it if it came down to it. The last thing he wanted was to finally get back into a human body only to have this monster immediately tear him apart. He had to find a way to defend himself against it.

It was surprisingly easy to read the thing's thoughts and memories. Warlock had been expecting some kind of resistance, some form of defense, but the thing was an open book. He wondered if his thoughts were just as transparent to the demon-dog? In the thing's memories, he saw its former life in hell, feeding on the ethereal ectoplasmic flesh of doomed souls. He saw how he'd been summoned to earth by those crazy Cuban devil-worshippers and how he'd eaten his way out of his mother's womb. He saw everything about the creature whose body he now shared… except how to kill it. There was nothing, outside of hell, the thing feared. And the things it feared in inferno were beings so terrifying that even Warlock found them difficult to look at. Creatures so vast, so hideous and powerful, their image shook him to his core.

Is that what the fuck hell is going to be like?

He had no doubt that he was headed to hell when he died and he could not imagine an existence populated with things like what he'd seen in the demon's mind. In hell, even this monstrous thing had predators, but here on earth, it believed itself to be invincible and Warlock wasn't so sure the thing was wrong.

Warlock still did not have full command of his awkward new body. Each step felt like he was about to topple over onto his face, but the smell of flesh drew him down the hall where half the girls had barricaded themselves in a room. Someone had found Ms. Dorothy's keys and led the rest of the girls downstairs and out the front door. The remaining girls wept and sobbed and prayed. A window opened and set off the alarm. The girls began screaming for the police. That's when Warlock remembered the sirens. The police had surrounded the building. There was no avoiding it now, he was going to have to fight his way out and that meant revealing himself. He was kind of looking forward to it.

"This is the police! Throw down your weapons, release the hostages and come out with your hands where we can see 'em!"

Warlock looked down at the long hooked black talons jutting from his fingertips and chuckled, a deep, throaty, raspy sound that was more like a series of hoarse barks.

Throw down my weapons, huh? That's easier said than done.

***

A small group of women, dressed in pajamas, underwear, and bathrobes, came running out of the Harriet Tubman Home for Abused Women, screaming bloody murder. Demetrius noticed, despite the tense situation, that some of them were kind of hot. He wondered if Warlock had noticed too and that immediately took his mind to an image of that gruesome, gargoyle-faced dog, with its paws locked around one of these bitches' waist, pounding its hairy doggy dick in her from behind. Demetrius felt bile rise in his throat. He fought the image out of his mind with some difficulty.

The police were so nervous they nearly opened fire on the women as they fled the shelter. The SWAT team captain had to yell, "Hold your fire!" when the sound of several dozen safeties clicking off at once was immediately followed by the sound of hammers being cocked back. The girls stopped in their tracks. They knew the sound as well.

A couple SWAT team officers ran over with their riot shields raised to collect the girls and hurry them across the yard, behind the line of parked police vehicles. Detective Dom stood waiting for them with Salvadore's grandma, still in her tight-fitting EMT uniform, making a rather pathetic show of examining the girls. She didn't even have a stethoscope or so much as a band aid. She looked in their eyes with a little penlight as they ran up to her, checked their pulse, acknowledged any cuts or bruises without treating them then went on to the next one. Demetrius shook his head. She must be magical if she was able to pull off this charade. Any fool could tell the old bitch didn't know a damn thing about medicine.

The women were still screaming and crying as the detective tried to probe them for information.

"How many of them are there?"

"Just one! There's just one of them. It's some kind of fucking monster! It was a dog, then we locked it in the closet, then it turned into this fucking werewolf or weredog or something. It killed her! It ripped her guts out!"

The first girl to speak up was a young hoodrat with curlers in her hair. She was only wearing a bra and panties and they were barely holding her in. Her ass was amazing, like a beachball split down the middle, and her titties looked like what a stripper would have paid a plastic surgeon thousands of dollars for. But it was obvious by the way they jiggled with her slightest movement and by her situation (ain't no way this broke-ass bitch could have afforded fake ones) that they were real. Demetrius stared at her titties the entire time she was talking to the detective. He moved in closer so he could hear more and to get a better look at her body.

If I was Warlock, I damn-sure would have fucked this fine-ass bitch. I ain't normally about raping bitches but goddamn! he thought.

"Okay. Okay. Calm down. Who did he kill?" The detective asked.

"It killed her! It wasn't a damn person! It talked like a man, but that wasn't no fuckin' man. It was some kind of dog-thing. How the hell did that thing talk? It killed Ms Dorothy and I think Missy's dead too. It ripped her arm off.

71

It kept saying it was going to kill all of us. How can that thing talk?"

"Is he armed? What kind of weapon does he have?"

"It's not a fucking HE! Ain't you listening, fool? It's got claws! Big fucking claws!"

"And fangs!" one of the other girls added.

The detective nodded and then passed both girls over to one of the uniformed officers. He obviously thought she was hysterical. He tried to question a couple of the other women with the same result. Finally, he spoke to one of the guys from SWAT who was holding a bullhorn. The guy nodded then put the bullhorn to his lips.

"You've got some injured people in there! I'd like to send in a couple of paramedics. Once we make sure everyone is okay, then we can talk!"

There was no reply except for the alarm and the screaming of the women still trapped inside with Warlock. Demetrius kept thinking about what that ghetto bitch with the big ass and titties told the detective about the dog transforming into a werewolf-dog-thing. He looked over at Salvador's grandmother and saw fear in her eyes. No. It was more than fear. There was sheer terror in her eyes. She stared at the hoodrat like the woman had just told her the world was ending. When the old woman turned to look at the house, she flinched as if she was expecting it to attack her. It was clear that she knew exactly what the woman was talking about and whatever it was that Warlock had turned into had this crazy-old bitch spooked.

Shit. What the fuck am I supposed to do now? Demetrius wondered. He strongly considered just creepin'-tha-fuck-away.

But what if Warlock manages to get away from these cops? If he finds out I bailed on his ass he'll come fuck me up.

That thought kept Demetrius right where he was. Like it or not, he was in it 'til the end.

There was a loud bang, like a door being kicked open, followed by snarls and growls. It sounded like a dogfight in there. The screams from the women grew louder and more frantic. Another loud bang and the alarm went silent.

The SWAT team started to move, charging across the lawn. One of them was about to toss a concussion grenade through the window when a voice like something from hell emanated from the dark interior of the house.

"IF ANYONE COMES INTO THIS HOUSE, EVERYONE WILL DIE! EVERYONE! GET THOSE SWAT MUTHERFUCKERS BACK! NOW!!!"

All the cops froze. The words were perfectly clear, but the voice was completely inhuman.

Oh fuck. What the fuck am I going to do? This motherfucker is about to go to war with the whole damn Philly PD!

Once again, Demetrius considered cutting out, but again decided against it. Warlock didn't say he would kill the bitches in the house if the cops tried to break in. He said *everyone.* Meech looked out at the sea of police vehicles and cops, stretching up and down the block.

Could that nigga really kill all of them? he wondered. Warlock couldn't, but that thing he had become just might.

I am so fucked, Demetrius thought.

The cops retreated back across the yard. Snipers moved into position on neighboring buildings and in the two trees closest to the Tubman Home. They looked obvious as fuck sitting in the trees and Meech was sure that if he could spot them then Warlock damn sure could.

"MEECH!"

Oh, fuck.

"MEECH! ARE YOU OUT THERE, NIGGA? YOU'D BETTER ANSWER ME! I WANT YOU AND THOSE CUBAN MOTHERFUCKERS IN HERE NOW! AND I WANT DETECTIVE DOM!"

"Shit!" Meech yelled. He looked over at Salvador who was still sitting in the ambulance, bobbing his head and listening to a pair of headphones. He was obviously high. He must have gotten into whatever drugs the EMTs kept in there, morphine most likely or something close.

"Fuck!"

73

Demetrius walked over to the detective, who looked confused.

"I'm Demetrius...uh... Meech. He's talking about me and her," he said, pointing a thumb toward Salvador's grandmother. She cast him a murderous gaze in response.

"Okay, what the fuck is going on here?"

"You wouldn't believe me if I told you, but everything those girls said is true. That thing in there? It ain't even close to being human. I don't know if any of us is coming back out if we go in there."

The detective stared into Demetrius's eyes with his mouth open as if he was looking for the right words but couldn't find them.

"You're all crazy."

"You're crazy if you go in there. I ain't got a choice and neither does she. This is our fault and we need to fix it. But there ain't no reason for your ass to go in there. I'm tellin' you this and I don't even like fuckin' cops."

"Well, thanks for the warning, *homeboy.* But it's my fucking *job!* Now, tell me how you two are involved."

"We created it. *She* created it. She put some kind of spell on my dog and did some kind of voodoo surgery on it. It gave birth to that thing in there. It gets complicated after that, but that voice you hear? That's Warlock. He borrowed the dog from me and now his soul is trapped inside of it."

"Warlock? That's Warlock in there? The fucking killer-for-hire?" A gleam leapt into the detective's eyes. "I've been trying to catch that piece of shit since I made detective. He's in there with some kind of attack dog? Well, that explains it."

"No. That's not what I said. He *is* the damn dog!"

"You two stay right here!"

The detective jogged over to another group of detectives to confer with them, leaving Demetrius alone with the old woman.

"Lo que el fuck están haciendo? ¿Por qué decirle todo?" the old woman asked. It was apparent, from her tone, that she was not pleased. Pissed-da-fuck-off was more like it.

"I don't know what the fuck you just said" Demetrius

replied.

The old woman traced a symbol in the air with her middle finger. This time, when she spoke, it looked again like she was being voice-dubbed.

"I said, what the fuck are you doing? Why did you tell that fucking cop everything?"

"Because it don't fuckin' matter no more. Whatever you and Salvador have been whispering about, whatever you two are so afraid of, is happening right now. Did you hear what that bitch with the big titties said? Warlock is changing into something. Whatever it is he's turning into, I can tell that it scares the shit out of you. So, we ain't got no choice. We have to stop it now. And we can't do that shit from out here. We need to get in there with that detective. I'm just hoping that once we get Warlock out of that thing, that you know how to kill it because he's probably the only thing holding it back right now. Once his mind ain't in control of it no more, I think shit is going to hit the fan. I think you do to. So, can you kill it?"

The old woman looked down at her feet and shook her head.

"I don't know. Maybe."

"What?"

"I said maybe."

"Fucking, maybe? That's all tha-fuck you got?"

"This has never happened before. It's never gone this far. The demon has matured now. It's grown and gotten stronger. I don't know if my spells will still work on it."

"It's only been a couple days!"

"They usually only last one night. We use them and then send them back. You fucked everything up when you gave it to Warlock and let it eat him."

"Fuck. Fuck. FUCK! I'm going to fucking die. I knew it the minute I saw that thing tear out of Sheba's belly. I'm a fucking dead man."

"GET YOUR ASS IN HERE, MEECH! IF DETECTIVE DOM ISN'T IN HERE IN FIVE MINUTES WITH DEMETRIUS AND THE CUBANS, I START SENDING

THESE BITCHES OUT ONE PIECE AT A TIME!"

Even without amplification Warlock's voice was louder than the bullhorn.

Detective Dom walked up behind Demetrius with two bullet proof vests.

"Put these on."

He had taken off the borrowed EMT uniform and was now wearing a blue shirt with the sleeves rolled up under a vest that looked lighter and newer then the ones he handed to Demetrius and the old Cuban woman. He also wore a riot helmet. Demetrius took the vests. They felt like they weighed fifty pounds each.

"Oh thanks. This will help. I'll be dead and uncomfortable."

"Just put them the fuck on!"

"Yes, sir!" Demetrius answered.

Detective Dom grabbed the bullhorn from the SWAT captain, a hard, lean man in his forties with a crewcut that was turning gray at the temples and small, narrow eyes sunk back in his skull. The detective leaned in close to the captain's ear.

"If I can get the suspect near the window are you sure your guys can take him out?"

"You know the answer to that. You get this freak where we can see him and I don't care what he's on, we'll take him out."

They brought a couple large spotlights forward and lit up the front of the house. That was the cue for them to head into the house.

"Warlock! We're coming in!" The detective handed the bullhorn back to the captain.

"Here." He handed Demetrius and the old woman a couple of riot helmets. Demetrius felt ridiculous, but he put it on. He imagined his head still inside it when Warlock ripped it off. The three of them began the long walk across the yard to the Harriet Tubman Home for Abused Women.

***

What was left of the women were huddled in one corner of the room. Warlock had been unable to control himself and had murdered two more of them. One of them tried to fight him off when he busted through the door. She'd come at him with a chair. Warlock swatted it aside then smacked her to the floor. The other girl had shattered the window and tried to climb out of it. He snatched her back inside and strangled her unconscious. That's when his animal nature took over and the beast he'd felt growing inside of him, the demon whose ghastly fantasies he'd seen in his head, came out.

Warlock tore off the woman's clothes along with some of her skin. She was a large woman, Puerto Rican or Italian or some combination of both. She had huge fat breasts that sagged down to her belly. Warlock had always liked his women plump. Her hips were wide and curvaceous, giving the lower half of her body the shape of a heart. Warlock squeezed them. His claws punched through the skin into the supple fat tissue, drawing blood. Seeing the blood aroused the demon further. He bent down to suck on the plump nipple but his new mouth wouldn't work right. He couldn't purse his canine lips. Instead, he lapped at them a bit, drooling over them with his long thick tongue before biting into them. Once he tasted the sweet flesh any semblance of control evaporated. The remaining girls screamed and prayed as he tore the woman's massive fat mammaries from her chest and devoured them in a few quick gulps. The woman woke up when she felt the first bite, crying, screaming, and punching at Warlock's head as he tore into her, but she quickly lost conscious again before the last of her breasts disappeared down Warlock's gullet. Warlock lapped at the woman's bare ribcage, drinking her blood, coating his face in her life-fluid, growling low in his throat.

His hairy penis was now fully erect, excited by the violence. A long purplish shaft that resembled a normal human cock extended another six inches from its fur-covered foreskin. He rolled the large woman over onto her belly and mounted her from behind, fucking her savagely, doggy-style. He bit her on the back of the neck for leverage so he could pound deeper into her. He underestimated the strength in his new jaws and his fangs sliced through her neck and crunched her cervical vertebrae. The woman's head fell off and rolled across the floor just as he reached orgasm. He was still cumming in the fat woman's corpse when the police began barking at him again with that damn bullhorn. That's when he spotted the SWAT team charging across the front lawn. He tossed the decapitated woman aside and roared in a voice that shook the room, telling them to stay back. Then he looked at what he'd done and was horrified. He was losing it. The demon was taking over. It was time to get this done with. He called out to the police to bring him Demetrius, Detective Victor Dom, and the Cubans. He needed to end this shit now.

There were three girls left, huddled in one corner of the room. The demon was again, filling Warlock's mind with visions of rape and carnage. It was a struggle to keep his mind on the trio walking across the lawn toward the house. The demon seemed unconcerned with them, neither threatened nor particularly interested. Nothing seemed to interest it but killing, eating, and fucking, preferably simultaneously. Warlock turned and growled at the three women.

"You stay here. Any of you move and you'll get to feel what your fat friend felt."

"Candy. Her name was Candice," said a bony little red-headed white girl with pimples and freckles in equal number. She had streaks of mascara running down her cheeks from crying. She looked like a raccoon.

"I don't give a fuck what her name was and I don't care who you are either," He pointed one long taloned finger at her. "If anyone moves, you're next but I'll make sure you stay alive until I'm finished with you."

Warlock turned and walked out into the hall to greet his guests.

***

The house was dark. The front door still hung open from when the women had fled from the house. There was no need to knock, but they did anyway.

"Hello? We're here!"

"Come in." The voice was lower now, not as threatening, almost seductive. It came from somewhere upstairs.

The old woman pulled a dried crow's foot from her purse and scratched her wrist with it. Then she scratched the front door. She pulled out a vial and sprinkled a fine white powder across the threshold then she stepped across it and shut the door behind her.

"What was that?" Demetrius asked.

"If we don't come out, it can't either."

"You mean if *you* don't come out. You only put *your* blood on the door."

"What does it matter?"

"Shhh!" The detective said, "I hear something."

They listened. They could hear women crying and a sound like something enormous breathing.

"How big is this dog?"

"Not a dog. Not anymore. It's a demon, a demon that walks like a man," said the old woman.

"Yeah, I'm about sick of that demon werewolf shit. Ain't nothing up there but a murderous thug and some kind of attack dog that you bred for him," the detective said.

"Believe what you want. You'll know soon enough."

They walked further into the house. Demetrius groped for a light switch. They felt their way down the hall and to the bottom of the stairs before Demetrius found the light switch and immediately wished he hadn't. Without shadows to hide his features, Demetrius was able to get a good look at the demonic thing Warlock had become. The metamorphosis had transformed him into some kind of dog-headed gargoyle sans wings. He had been prepared for something that looked like a werewolf. This thing looked nothing like a wolf. It had some of the features of a bullmastiff in its floppy jaws and short fur but its teeth were massive sabers that jutted out from its mouth like the tusks of a wild boar only they protruded from both the top and bottom jaws, four in all. The eyes were so human it was disturbing in such an inhuman face. The creature's arms and shoulders were almost completely human with muscles like a Masters of the Universe action figure. Its chest was still mostly that of a dog, however, as were its legs which sported huge muscular quadriceps ending in the backwards legs of a dog where its calves and shins should have been. Demetrius's brain wanted to shut down. He felt his vision narrow and his testicles shrink up into his stomach.

"What-tha-fuck? Warlock? Is that you?" Demetrius whispered.

"Who the fuck else would it be?"

"Dear God!" The detective shouted as he pulled his Glock from its holster.

"Detective Victor Dom. I am so happy you could join us."

Warlock charged down the stairs. Demetrius dropped to the floor and covered his head while the detective freed his weapon. The old woman, Salvador's grandma, had retreated back into the hallway. She was rummaging in her purse, pulling out various dried animal parts, a cobra's head, the crow's foot, what looked like the dried head of a vulture, and something that resembled an embalmed pig fetus but had eyes that made Demetrius think of a human fetus. She placed them in a circle then pulled out the vial of white powder and drew lines from one dried thing to the next. Then she began drawing designs inside the circle in what looked like some kind of handwriting but in a language Demetrius couldn't make out. He assumed it was Spanish, but it didn't look like any kind of Spanish he'd ever seen. The old woman pulled out a knife, slit her wrist, and dripped her own blood onto the collection of dried things, all the while ignoring the battle taking place on the stairs. It wasn't much of a battle anyway. The detective didn't stand a chance against Warlock.

Detective Dom was a great shot. But Warlock was on

top of him before he could get off a single round. Demetrius had never seen anything move that fast. Warlock grabbed the detective by the wrists and twisted the gun from his hands. He was being extremely gentle, trying his best not to damage the man's body. The detective was the only one in the room who didn't know why.

"I want to kill you so bad I'm about to bust a nut all over you. You don't know how fucking lucky you are that I need your body."

"My body? You're not going to... your're not gonna..."

"Don't flatter yourself, Victor. I ain't gonna fuck you. I'm going to possess you." He turned toward Demetrius who was still curled up on the floor trying not to scream.

"Where the fuck is Salvador?"

"He... h-he's outside, high as fuck as usual. I- I brought his grandma. She's the only one who can do this shit."

Warlock turned toward the old lady. It was obvious that he recognized her. "Are you ready over there?"

"Almost." The old woman replied. Her lips still moved differently than the words that were coming out of it. It would have been creepy as fuck under normal circumstances. But it was probably the least disturbing thing about this evening.

"What are you going to do to me?" The detective asked. Warlock was still holding him by both wrists and he'd driven the detective down to his knees, twisting the wrists just hard enough to cause pain without snapping the joints.

"I'm going to tear out your fucking soul."

"Ya'll better hurry. If the rest of the cops don't hear from the detective soon they'll be bustin' in here."

"It's ready," the old lady said. "Bring him in here.'

Warlock dragged the detective into the hallway then lifted him into the circle with him.

"Where do I stand?"

"Right there in the circle where you are."

"What are you doing? What are you going to do to me?"

"Shhhh! If you scream I'll have to kill you, Victor. I don't really want to do that but you know damn well I will."

The detective fell silent. The old woman began to chant.

This time, it didn't sound like either English or Spanish. She stepped into the circle, grabbed Warlock by the wrist, and slit it open with the knife.

"He needs to drink it."

"No fucking way!"

Warlock grabbed detective Victor Dom by the throat and squeezed until the detective's tongue lolled from his open mouth and his eyes rolled up in his head, then he pressed his wrist to the detective's slack lips and dribbled his blood down his throat.

The old woman's prayer's and chants rose in volume and speed. She began to dance, shouting incantations in that same incomprehensible language. Demetrius looked nervously back toward the open door, expecting her yelling to bring the entire SWAT team

"Can't we hurry this shit up?

"He must drink more blood," the old woman replied.

Warlock pulled his wrist away from the detective's mouth and bit into it himself, tearing a huge avulsion in his forearm. Blood sprayed like an open faucet. This time, the detective drowned in the arterial spray.

A full minute passed. Then another. And another. Demetrius glanced out the door, and saw the SWAT team begin to mobilize again outside.

"Fuck, man! They're coming!"

Warlock and the detective suddenly collapsed. The old woman continued her chanting, waving the crow's foot over the two prone forms. Demetrius could have sworn the he saw the pig fetus begin to move. The next few seconds passed by in a blur.

The detective stood up. He staggered, like he was drunk, then stared at his hands and began to laugh. Next, the huge dog-demon-thing stood up and the detective ran out of the circle with the creature close behind him. Its face looked different now. The gleam of intelligence in its eyes was gone. In its place was a maniacal radiance, a burning hatred like twin stars. Warlock was gone, all that was left was the demon and it looked royally pissed.

A teargas grenade shattered a nearby window followed by a concussion grenade that blasted Demetrius' eardrums and blinded him with a flash of white phosphorous. He couldn't see, couldn't hear, his eyes, nose, throat, and lungs burned with tear gas, and somewhere in the room was a murderous demon that ate people like fucking Scooby snacks.

"Help! Somebody help me!"

Demetrius tripped and fell into something hard, something big, something covered in fur that growled like a muscle car engine. He felt a sharp pain as something bit into his neck and shoulder and jerked him off the floor. He felt himself being shook the way a dog would shake a chew toy. Then his flesh tore, his bones cracked and he fell to the floor with a large piece of him missing and warm fluid spurting from the wound.

His eyes cleared a bit and through the cloud of tear gas he could see the thing reaching down for him again. Beyond him, he saw the old woman, still chanting, the detective running out into the yard and the SWAT team charging through the open front door. Then he was staring into the creature's mouth at rows of razor sharp teeth, a tongue the size of a man's hand and a throat that looked as big as a storm drain.

Epilogue

Warlock stared at himself in the mirror. It was still hard to get used to the white skin and those ice-blue eyes. He brushed his teeth, splashed water on his face and took a few moments to practice his speech. He needed to get rid of his urban dialect. Victor Dom sounded more like a dago than a brotha. But he too had worked hard to get rid of his accent and the man's voice now sounded as flat and unaccented as he could make it, though that South Philly Italian swagger was still evident in his speech, especially when he was around his family.

Ever since he'd left the hospital, Warlock had been avoiding the detective's family, afraid they would notice that something wasn't right. He told them that he was tired, stressed, needed some time to himself, and they had obliged, leaving him alone in his bedroom or in his study. Warlock tried his best to familiarize himself with Victor's life. He spent all afternoon flipping through photo albums and watching videos of the family, memorizing names and faces and moments from the detective's past but more importantly, studying Victor's mannerisms, how he walked, how he talked, his facial expressions, his sense of humor, getting to know his hobbies. He felt like he knew the man pretty well by the time the sun set but still wasn't sure he did a good enough Victor Dom impersonation to fool his wife. He couldn't hide from her much longer.

He left the bathroom and walked across the hall into his study. He saw Victor's wife and kids in the living room and they saw him. His wife smiled at him and Warlock smiled back before he shut the door and locked it.

"Fuck."

He knew he couldn't avoid her forever but he had no idea how he was going to fool her. She'd notice that he kissed differently and when they got in the bedroom, she'd be in for a real shock. The one thing there were no videos of was how Victor got down in the bedroom. He didn't know how she'd react when he bent her over and fucked her doggystyle, slapping her ass and pulling her hair. He wasn't sure how she'd react if he didn't. He didn't even know if they still fucked.

Warlock removed a pipe from the drawer of a large mahogany desk that had once belonged to Detective Victor Dom, along with the 3,000 square foot house and the 2010 Lincoln Navigator and the wife with the big fake tits and collagen injected, dick-sucking lips and the two blonde-haired boys and the little pug dog and the Persian cat. It was all his now and all he had to do was convince them that that he was still Victor Dom. He leaned back and let out a long sigh, staring up at the coffered ceiling with its ornate crown molding. Victor lived like a fucking king and it was all his now.

Warlock stood up and walked back and forth across the room with the pipe in his hand, practicing Victor's walk. Heel. Toe. Heel. Toe. Like a fucking runway model or something. He practiced lighting his pipe the way he'd seen Victor light it over and over again in video after video. He hadn't known the man smoked a pipe until he'd watched the video. He never smoked in public when he was on duty. Warlock had watched the man enough times through his rifle scope. He was glad that he'd watched the video or else he might have tripped himself up if someone offered to bring him his pipe. He hated the fucking things himself. Pipe tobacco smelled like hot ass to him. If he had it his way, he'd have packed it with weed instead. But it was one of the things he'd have to get used to. Maybe he'd announce to the family that he was quitting, getting healthy. He could tell them that almost dying last night had given him a new perspective on life and he was going to give up smoking and start eating right. He'd just have to sneak out every now and again for soul food.

He popped another DVD into the computer. This one was of a barbecue. It was Victor's 35th birthday party. The man had been ten years younger than Warlock. He'd not only gotten a new body and a new life but Warlock had apparently gotten a ten-year life extension. He laughed at his good luck. Even though it had been hell trapped in that demon's hideous fucking body, it had all turned out alright, better than alright. Victor even had a bigger dick than Warlock had and he was anxious to try it out on the detective's wife.

Well, I can't hide in here forever. Time to make my appearance and see if I can pull this shit off.

He stood up from the desk and started toward the door when the window behind him shattered and something huge leapt through it into the room. He didn't even have to guess who and what it was.

"Meech! What the fuck are you doing here?! You're about to fuck everything up!" Warlock whispered.

Demetrius looked like shit. The demon's body was riddled with bullet wounds. One eye was missing and its left shoulder slumped from where a bullet had shattered its collarbone.

"I want my old body back!"

"Well what tha fuck did you come here for?! The damn demon ate that shit! Your ass is stuck now. It killed the old lady too. Ain't nobody to turn you back now."

"Salvador thinks he can do it. He just needs a body to put me in."

"Well, what the fuck do you want me to do? I can't help you."

"Honey? Are you okay in there? What was that noise?"

"That's my wife... I mean, Victor's wife. If she sees you, this shit is over. We're both fucked. What's left of the Philly PD is out after you. I'll be damned if they gonna find your ass here. Now, get tha fuck outta here!"

Warlock grabbed Denmetrius' arm and the big demon growled. Warlock jerked his hand away.

"Come on, fool. We ain't got time for this bullshit. Get your ass outta here."

"I ain't goin' nowhere."

"Honey? Honey? I heard a crash. Let me in. I'm worried!"

"I always wondered what life would be like as a woman."

"Awww, hell no. That's just sick, you fucking pervert."

Demetrius shrugged his big demon shoulder. The one with the shattered clavicle didn't move.

"Why should you be the only one who gets a new life? I want to live in the suburbs in a big ass house too."

"As a bitch though? You some kind of fag?"

Demetrius shrugged again.

"I don't know. I've never tried dick before. Maybe I'll like it."

"Well, I ain't fuckin'you!"

"I'm just kidding with you. Maybe I'll become a lesbian. We could have a marriage of convenience. Just open the damn door. I want you to introduce me to the missus."

Warlock walked over to the door, already convincing himself that it wouldn't be such a bad thing having Demetrius as a wife. At least he wouldn't have to worry about whether he kissed right or not. If he was lucky, the demon would eat the bitch as soon as the transfer was complete. Then he'd be single again. Warlock smiled and opened the door.

"Come on in, sweetheart"

Mrs. Dom stepped into the den and screamed.

WRATH JAMES WHITE is the author of *The Resurrectionist, Succulent Prey, Yacob's Curse, Sacrifice, Pure Hate,* and *Prey Drive (Succulent Prey Part II).* He is also the author of *Voracious, To The Death, Skinzz, The Reaper, Like Porno for Psychos, Everyone Dies Famous In A Small Town, The Book of a Thousand Sins, His Pain,* and *Population Zero.* He is the co-author of *Teratologist* co-written with the king of extreme horror, Edward Lee, *Orgy of Souls* co-written with Maurice Broaddus, *The Killings* and *Hero* co-written with J.F. Gonzalez, *Son of a Bitch* co-written with Andre Duza and *Poisoning Eros I and II* co-written with Monica J. O'Rourke.

His short stories have appeared in several dozen magazines and anthologies. In 2010 his poetry collection, *Vicious Romantic* was nominated for a Bram Stoker Award.

Wrath lives and works in Austin, Texas with his two daughters, Isis and Nala, his son Sultan and his lovely wife, Christie White.

ANDRE DUZA is an actor, stuntman, and a leading member of the Bizarro movement in contemporary literary fiction. His writing has been described as horrific, bizarre, smart, funny, and fast-paced, with lush, finely-detailed prose. He is fond of collaborating with artists (both unknown and established) to create macabre illustrations for his books.

Andre's novels include *Dead Bitch Army, Jesus Freaks, Necro Sex Machine,* his graphic novel, *Hollow-Eyed Mary,* and the Star Trek comic *Outer Light*, co-written with writer/ producer Morgan Gendel. He recently penned the graphic novel adaptation of the upcoming Singaporean Horror film, *Afterimages.* He is currently collaborating on a novel *Voodoo Chile* with author Wayne Simmons.

Andre has also contributed to such collections and anthologies as *Book of Lists: Horror, The Bizarro Starter Kit, Undead,* and *Undead: Flesh Feast.*

In his other life, Andre works as a Certified Personal Trainer and a Kung Fu Instructor.

deadite
press

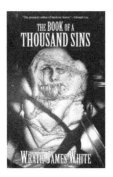

"The Book of a Thousand Sins" Wrath James White - Welcome to a world of Zombie nymphomaniacs, psychopathic deities, voodoo surgery, and murderous priests. Where mutilation sex clubs are in vogue and torture machines are sex toys. No one makes it out alive – not even God himself.

"If Wrath James White doesn't make you cringe, you must be riding in the wrong end of a hearse."
       -Jack Ketchum

"Population Zero" Wrath James White - An intense sadistic tale of how one man will save the world through sterilization. *Population Zero* is the story of an environmental activist named Todd Hammerstein who is on a mission to save the planet. In just 50 years the population of the planet is expected to double. But not if Todd can help it. From Wrath James White, the celebrated master of sex and splatter, comes a tale of environmentalism, drugs, and genital mutilation.

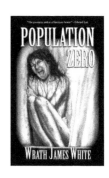

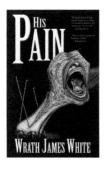

"His Pain" Wrath James White - Life is pain . . . . . . or at least it is for Jason. Born with a rare central nervous disorder, every sensation is pain. Every sound, scent, texture, flavor, even every breath, brings nothing but mind-numbing pain. Until the arrival of Yogi Arjunda of the Temple of Physical Enlightenment. He claims to be able to help Jason, to be able to give him a life of more than agony. But the treatment leaves Jason changed and he wants to share what he learned. He wants to share his pain . . . A novella of pain, pleasure, and transcendental splatter.

"The Vegan Revolution . . . with Zombies" David Agranoff - Thanks to a new miracle drug the cute little pig no longer feels a thing as she is led to the slaughter. The only problem? Once the drug enters the food supply anyone who eats it is infected. From fast food burgers to free-range organic eggs, eating animal products turns people into shambling brain-dead zombies – not even vegetarians are safe!
"A perfect blend of horror, humor and animal activism."
       - Gina Ranalli

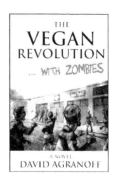

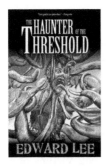

"The Haunter of the Threshold" Edward Lee - There is something very wrong with this backwater town. Suicide notes, magic gems, and haunted cabins await her. Plus the woods are filled with monsters, both human and otherworldly. And then there are the horrible tentacles . . . Soon Hazel is thrown into a battle for her life that will test her sanity and sex drive. The sequel to H.P. Lovecraft's The Haunter of the Dark is Edward Lee's most pornographic novel to date!

"The Innswich Horror" Edward Lee - In July, 1939, antiquarian and H.P. Lovecraft aficionado, Foster Morley, takes a scenic bus tour through northern Massachusetts and finds Innswich Point. There far too many similarities between this fishing village and the fictional town of Lovecraft's masterpiece, The Shadow Over Innsmouth. Join splatter king Edward Lee for a private tour of Innswich Point - a town founded on perversion, torture, and abominations from the sea.

"Mangled Meat" Edward Lee - No writer is more hardcore, offensive, or notorious than Edward Lee. His world is one of torture, bizarre fetishes, and alien autopsies. Prepare yourself, as these three novellas from the king of splatterspunk are guaranteed to make you gasp, gag, and laugh your ass off. Featuring "The Decortication Technician," "The Cyesolagniac," and "Room 415."

"Necro Sex Machine" Andre Duza - America post apocalypse...a toxic wasteland populated by bloodthristy scavengers, mutated animals, and roving bands of organized militias wing for control of civilized society's leftovers. Housed in small settlements that pepper the wasteland, the survivors of the third world war struggle to rebuild amidst the scourge of sickness and disease and the constant threat of attack from the horrors that roam beyond their borders. But something much worse has risen from the toxic fog.

THE VERY BEST IN CULT HORROR

deadite press

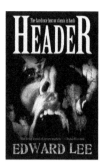

"Header" Edward Lee - In the dark backwoods, where law enforcement doesn't dare tread, there exists a special type of revenge. Something so awful that it is only whispered about. Something so terrible that few believe it is real. Stewart Cummings is a government agent whose life is going to Hell. His wife is ill and to pay for her medication he turns to bootlegging. But things will get much worse when bodies begin showing up in his sleepy small town. Victims of an act known only as "a Header."

"Red Sky" Nate Southard - When a bank job goes horrifically wrong, career criminal Danny Black leads his crew from El Paso into the deserts of New Mexico in a desperate bid for escape. Danny soon finds himself with no choice but to hole up in an abandoned factory, the former home of Red Sky Manufacturing. Danny and his crew aren't the only living things in Red Sky, though. Something waits in the abandoned factory's shadows, something horrible and violent. Something hungry. And when the sun drops, it will feast.

"Zombies and Shit" Carlton Mellick III - Twenty people wake to find themselves in a boarded-up building in the middle of the zombie wasteland. They soon discover they have been chosen as contestants on a popular reality show called Zombie Survival. Each contestant is given a backpack of supplies and a unique weapon. Their goal: be the first to make it through the zombie-plagued city to the pick-up zone alive. But because there's only one seat available on the helicopter, the contestants not only have to fight against the hordes of the living dead, they must also fight each other.

"All You Can Eat" Shane McKenzie - Deep in Texas there is a Chinese restaurant that harbors a secret. Its food is delicious and the secret ingredient ensures that once you have one bite you'll never be able to stop. But when the food runs out and the customers turn to cannibalism, the kitchen staff must take up arms against these obese people-eaters or else be next on the menu!

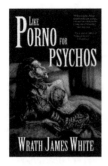
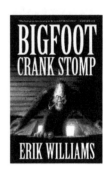

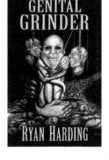

deadite press

"Earthworm Gods" Brian Keene - One day, it starts raining-and never stops. Global super-storms decimate the planet, eradicating most of mankind. Pockets of survivors gather on mountaintops, watching as the waters climb higher and higher. But as the tides rise, something else is rising, too. Now, in the midst of an ecological nightmare, the remnants of humanity face a new menace, in a battle that stretches from the rooftops of submerged cities to the mountaintop islands jutting from the sea. The old gods are dead. Now is the time of the Earthworm Gods...

"Earworm Gods: Selected Scenes from the End of the World" Brian Keene - a collection of short stories set in the world of Earthworm Gods and Earthworm Gods II: Deluge. From the first drop of rain to humanity's last waterlogged stand, these tales chronicle the fall of man against a horrifying, unstoppable evil. And as the waters rise over the United States, the United Kingdom, Australia, New Zealand, and elsewhere-brand new monsters surface-along with some familiar old favorites, to wreak havoc on an already devastated mankind..

"An Occurrence in Crazy Bear Valley" Brian Keene- The Old West has never been weirder or wilder than it has in the hands of master horror writer Brian Keene. Morgan and his gang are on the run--from their pasts and from the posse riding hot on their heels, intent on seeing them hang. But when they take refuge in Crazy Bear Valley, their flight becomes a siege as they find themselves battling a legendary race of monstrous, bloodthirsty beings. Now, Morgan and his gang aren't worried about hanging. They just want to live to see the dawn.

"Muerte Con Carne" Shane McKenzie - Human flesh tacos, hardcore wrestling, and angry cannibal Mexicans, Welcome to the Border! Felix and Marta came to Mexico to film a documentary on illegal immigration. When Marta suddenly goes missing, Felix must find his lost love in the small border town. A dangerous place housing corrupt cops, borderline maniacs, and something much more worse than drug gangs, something to do with a strange Mexican food cart…

"Jack's Magic Beans" Brian Keene - It happens in a split-second. One moment, customers are happily shopping in the Save-A-Lot grocery store. The next instant, they are transformed into bloodthirsty psychotics, interested only in slaughtering one another and committing unimaginably atrocious and frenzied acts of violent depravity. Deadite Press is proud to bring one of Brian Keene's bleakest and most violent novellas back into print once more. This edition also includes four bonus short stories:

"Whargoul" Dave Brockie - It is a beast born in bullets and shrapnel, feeding off of pain, misery, and hard drugs. Cursed to wander the Earth without the hope of death, it is reborn again and again to spread the gospel of hate, abuse, and genocide. But what if it's not the only monster out there? What if there's something worse? From Dave Brockie, the twisted genius behind GWAR, comes a novel about the darkest days of the twentieth century.

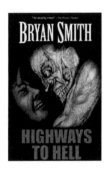

"Highways to Hell" Bryan Smith - The road to hell is paved with angels and demons. Brain worms and dead prostitutes. Serial killers and frustrated writers. Zombies and Rock 'n Roll. And once you start down this path, there is no going back. Collecting thirteen tales of shock and terror from Bryan Smith, Highways to Hell is a non-stop road-trip of cruelty, pain, and death. Grab a seat, Smith has such sights to show you.

"Apeshit" Carlton Mellick III - Friday the 13th meets Visitor Q. Six hipster teens go to a cabin in the woods inhabited by a deformed killer. An incredibly fucked-up parody of B-horror movies with a bizarro slant
"The new gold standard in unstoppable fetus-fucking kill-freakomania . . . Genuine all-meat hardcore horror meets unadulterated Bizarro brainwarp strangeness. The results are beyond jaw-dropping, and fill me with pure, unforgivable joy." - John Skipp

AVAILABLE FROM AMAZON.COM

Lightning Source UK Ltd.
Milton Keynes UK
UKHW050836250521
384274UK00007B/389